"Megan, we can't change the things that happen."

There was a strange light in his eyes as they held hers. "But people and perceptions can change. Do you believe that?"

"I don't know."

"We had something good starting for us. Why does *that* have to change?" Roan asked raggedly. He looked at her for what seemed a long time, then he closed the gap between them and held her in his arms.

She loved Roan and was about to reach up her arms to him when the realization hit her so suddenly that she flinched. How in heaven could she have forgotten even for a moment that the man who had kissed and caressed her was also the man she was forbidden to love?

She heard the raw hiss of breath. "Do you think by pushing me from you that you can wreak your own kind of revenge?"

Books by Rosemary Carter

ROSEMARY CARTER

letter from bronze mountain

Harlequin Books

TORONTO • NEW YORK • LONDON
AMSTERDAM • PARIS • SYDNEY • HAMBURG
STOCKHOLM • ATHENS • TOKYO • MILAN

Harlequin Presents first edition January 1985
ISBN 0-373-10752-8

Original hardcover edition published in 1984
by Mills & Boon Limited

CHAPTER ONE

'BRONZE MOUNTAIN?' The stationmaster took his pipe from his mouth and scratched his head. 'Won't get there today, miss.'

Green eyes looked up at him, puzzled. 'I thought there was a bus,' Megan said.

'Went yesterday.'

Megan watched as the train gathered speed and vanished in the lush pine forests of the Eastern Transvaal. 'When is the next bus?'

'Tomorrow.'

'Impulsive,' her mother had reproached her. 'You're so impulsive, Megan dear. Why don't you wait for a reply to your letter?'

Which might have taken a week or more to arrive. A week out of the precious six she had had to spare. Having made up her mind, Megan had been in no mood to wait. A little ruefully she shook her head now, and admitted to herself that her mother might have been right.

'Is there somewhere I can stay until tomorrow?' she asked.

The weathered face of the stationmaster was reflective. 'There's a hotel in the village.'

'Call that crumbling dump a hotel?' a low laughing voice asked.

Megan turned her head in the direction of the voice, as the stationmaster said, 'Now, Roan, you know it's the best we can offer till your fancy resort at Bronze Mountain is ready.'

Megan was aware of an odd quiver as she tilted back her head to look at the tall man who had come up behind them. He was in his early thirties, and his face was as attractive as his voice. His hair was dark, as were the eyes that had small laughter lines around them. There was something both intelligent and sensuous in the lean tanned features. The most dynamic man she had ever met, Megan decided in just five seconds.

She found her voice. 'You're from Bronze Mountain?'

'I am.'

'That's where I'm going.'

He looked down at her thoughtfully. 'I didn't know someone new was expected at the resort. Usually we arrange for people to be met.'

'It seems I chose the wrong day,' Megan said, without explaining that she had not waited long enough for arrangements to be made.

Should she ask him for a lift? She would if he did not make the offer of his own accord. A brief look in the direction of the village did not inspire her with the desire to spend a day killing time there.

'You've come by car, Roan?' the stationmaster asked.

The two men exchanged a glance, and then Roan said, 'Horseback. I just dropped by to see if my parcel had arrived.'

' 'Fraid not.'

'I'll come again.' Roan turned to Megan. 'I'll get someone to drive down and fetch you.'

She gave a smile of relief. 'Thank you.'

'Might not be till the evening, though, I won't get back to Bronze Mountain until then.'

So it would have to be either the station or the crumbling dump for her after all. A place where she could leave her luggage a while. Unpromising though the village appeared from this distance, perhaps there was somewhere she could walk, some place she could explore.

She watched Roan walk away, supple and lithe, as she had sensed he would be. At the end of the short platform he stopped and turned.

'You *could* come with me.'

Gladly she said, 'I could?'

'If you don't mind sharing a saddle with me.'

The idea of sharing a saddle with him was inexplicably exciting. Am I crazy? Megan wondered. I've just met the man, I don't react this way usually.

But nothing about the situation was usual. She should have waited for a reply to her letter, perhaps her mother had been right about that. Just as she should now tell Roan that she would wait for someone to fetch her by car.

'I don't mind at all.' She smiled up at him.

'Splendid.' He looked at her, really looked, as if he was taking in every detail of her appearance from smoky green eyes to upturned lips and smoothly curling hair the colour of pale honey. 'Splendid,' he said again, smiling back at her, and he sounded as if he meant it.

Megan felt her heart do an unaccountable little somersault in her chest, and then the stationmaster said, 'What about the luggage, Roan?' and her heartbeat returned to normal.

'No problem.' The tall man was unperturbed. 'You'll keep it here, won't you, Tom? Someone will come for it.'

Evidently Roan was a man of quick decisions. I like that, Megan thought. Henry, nice Henry whom she had decided not to marry after all, was a man who dithered when making the simplest decision: unfairly perhaps, it was a quality that had destroyed her confidence in him.

'I should tell you,' Roan said, 'that I'm not presently on

my way to Bronze Mountain. I've taken the day off. If you decide to come with me, you'll have to spend the day with me.'

A heart that had never somersaulted before that day performed the feat a second time in a minute. 'I don't mind that either,' Megan assured him.

Her luggage consisted of a suitcase containing her clothes and a smaller bag in which she had put, among other things, the sketches she would need. The sketches would be harder to replace than the clothes, and Megan watched as the stationmaster carried the two pieces into the small red-brick building.

'They'll be safe with me, miss,' he told her, and she smiled her thanks at him before following Roan.

At the back of the station a horse was tethered to a fence-post. A powerful animal, with strong flanks and a glossy-coat, it was pawing the ground with impatient hooves. At Roan's and Megan's approach it stood quite still for a moment, then threw back a beautiful head and let out a long whinnying sound.

Megan took a doubtful step backwards. 'Yours?' she queried.

'Mine. Thunder by name.'

'By appearance too. Looks wild.'

'Not in my hands.' He laughed, the sound low and vital. 'Don't be frightened, you'll be safe with me.'

'I know,' Megan murmured, and wondered how she knew it. Apart from the two facts that his name was Roan and that he seemed to work at Bronze Mountain, she really knew nothing about this tall stranger. It was unusual for Megan Westcott to put her trust in a man quite so quickly.

'Good,' he said, and there was a gleam of warmth in the dark brown eyes as he studied her face a moment. 'I'll help you up.'

He stepped towards her. She found herself noting the breadth of his shoulders beneath the brown shirt that matched the colour of his eyes. The top buttons of the shirt were open, revealing the thrust of a powerful neck and the dark hair that clung to a muscular chest.

As Roan swung her easily up on to the horse, Megan had no time to analyse the tingling sensation that his hands on her waist evoked, for then he was astride the beast too, and was telling her to hold on to him. After a long moment she did just that.

Thunder was already beginning to move when Roan turned his head and said, 'We haven't introduced ourselves.'

What a time for introductions! Megan laughed aloud. 'I know your name already, it's Roan. And I'm Megan.'

'Hello, Megan. Hold tight now, we're off.'

Megan clasped her hands demurely to Roan's waist, an adequate hold as the horse took the road outside the station at a sedate walk. And then they had left the station and the village behind them, and the horse gathered speed. With no thought of shame or demureness Megan let her arms go around Roan, and held on to him tightly.

Through the veld they sped, and the wild grass was long and swaying on all sides, and the wind tugged at her hair. The back of the man was hard against her chest, and the movement of the horse was rhythmic beneath her thighs. On the train Megan had wondered what the day would bring. She had rehearsed phrases in her mind, and had speculated on various situations, but nothing had prepared her for the reality of this ride. She laughed suddenly, joyfully, and knew the sound was muffled by Roan's broad back.

At the top of a hill Roan reined in the horse. 'Enjoy that?'

'Every moment!'

'A girl after my own heart.' She could not see his eyes, for it was not possible for him to turn his head quite so far, but she saw him smile, saw teeth that were white and strong against the rugged tan, saw the laughter lines crinkling around his lips, and again she felt a quiver that seemed to go right through her body.

'Is there a place you would like to see?' he asked.

'None in particular.'

'You know this part of the world?'

'It's my first visit.'

There were things she should have known, of course. Tammy might have written about this landscape, for in just ten minutes Megan already knew it was beautiful. Tammy might have described the scenery of the Lowveld, but that had not been her sister's way.

Tammy had written of the fun she was having. Of social evenings with the other workers at the resort. Of picnics and barbecues. Of men. Only one name remained in Megan's memory—Brendon Stevens. A wave of pain swept her. Firmly she pushed aside all thought of Brendon Stevens. There would be time to think about him later, at Bronze Mountain.

'Then you'll let me show you around?' There was an odd sound in Roan's voice, as if he sensed that her thoughts had been elsewhere, and wondered why.

'A conducted tour?' she asked.

'Something like it.' His tone was quiet. 'This was to have been a day for visiting my favourite spots.'

'You've been away?' She did not know what made her ask the question, except perhaps that there had been something in his tone that had suggested an absence.

After a moment he said, 'I've been away, yes.'

Still that quietness. A little uncertainly now, Megan said, 'I hope I won't be intruding.'

'Not at all. Actually, I'm glad of the company.'

A man like Roan would have as much company as he wanted, Megan reflected as the horse moved on to its master's command. She could not be the only woman who found him attractive. Attractive? She had met many attractive men in her twenty-three years. This man was something more. Dynamic was a word that she did not use easily, but it came to mind now. There was a compelling aura about Roan, a quality that was overwhelmingly male. Behind the laughter in his eyes she had sensed not only sensuousness, but strength and power as well.

And she wondered how in so short a time Megan Westcott, down-to-earth Megan, all her mother's talk of impulsiveness notwithstanding, could have formed so strong an opinion of a man. That had always been Tammy's way, not her sister's.

Willing herself not to think of Tammy—a time for thought and for the pain that inevitably accompanied it later, she wondered where Roan was taking her—and knew she did not care. The ride was a treat in itself.

She had known the Lowveld would be beautiful, but Tammy's postcards and the pictures she had seen in books of this area of South Africa's Eastern Transvaal had not prepared her fully for the beauty she saw all around her. Mountains and valleys, waterfalls leaping over shining heat-glazed rocks. And trees. Everywhere there were trees, for this was timber country.

Presently Roan slowed the horse, and Megan saw that they had come to a village. A very different village from the first one. At a walking pace the horse made its way along what seemed to be the main street, while Megan looked around her in bewilderment. She felt as if she had gone suddenly backwards in time, a feeling that was reinforced when Roan reined in outside what looked like an old-fashioned hotel, then vaulted lithely on to the ground.

'This is like a set in an old Western,' she remarked, looking down at him.

He grinned. 'You're not far off the mark.'

Reaching up his hands, he helped her down, and she wondered if it was the grin or the touch of his hands, or a combination of both, that set her pulses racing.

She watched him tether the horse to a hitching-post and then he said, 'Let's explore. Ever seen a ghost town, Megan?'

'Not off the movie screen.'

'This is one. You must have heard of Pilgrim's Rest?'

'The old gold-mining town?'

'Correct. And quite a tourist attraction it is today.' He grinned again, teeth white and strong against his tan. 'This little place is very similar. It's farther off the tourist track than Pilgrim's Rest, and though the houses have been preserved they haven't been restored. I enjoy walking here.'

Almost immediately Megan knew why. The village had a presence, a sense of history, of a time that had vanished when no more gold was to be found in the valley.

On the door of the hotel was a poster. It was tattered, but once it must have been bright and attractive and appealing. 'This must have been the focal point of social life here,' she mused.

'This together with the saloon.' Roan was close beside her, his voice reaching down to her was low and vital. 'On Saturday evenings the prospectors would ride into town and make for the hotel.'

'To celebrate their good fortune, I suppose.'

'Or to drown their sorrows. There was gold here, Megan, but only the lucky ones found it.'

Roan would have been one of the lucky ones, she thought. She could picture him as a prospector at the turn of the century, tall and tanned, tough and hard and sure of himself. He would have been one of those who found the gold. And on a Saturday night he'd have ridden into the village, looking for good drink and good company, neither of which would have been hard to find. The drink would have flowed freely for those with money to spend, and the women would have vied for his attention, drawn by the sexual appeal of this handsome man with the lithe muscled body and the rugged hard-planed face.

'Why do I get the feeling that you've gone back in time?'

She heard the teasing in his voice, but what struck her was his perceptiveness. There was very little that would escape this man.

'I did go back,' she admitted as they began to walk. 'Would you have liked to live here, Roan? Before the time of electricity and television and motor-cars?'

A brooding look came into his face. 'Perhaps. TV isn't my favourite form of entertainment, and as for mechanised transport—that isn't without its problems.' He paused a moment, then he said, 'Look, Megan this was the bakery. Did a thriving trade with all the men who had no wives to bake their bread for them.'

Megan would have loved to see inside the old shop, but it was locked, Roan told her. 'Doesn't matter,' she said, 'I've only to close my eyes to see those great ovens and the coals that were used to heat them. I can almost smell the new-baked bread.'

'You've a real sense of history,' he observed.

'I adore history.'

'We've something in common, then. I think you've a sense of romance too, Megan?'

There was something in the way he said the last words that sent the warmth rushing to her cheeks. Quickly she said, 'This must be the dispensary.'

'Right,' he agreed a little drily, as if he'd registered her haste to change the subject. 'A dispensary that existed before the days of antibiotics.'

They walked on. It was very quiet in the village. Truly a ghost village this, with not even the sigh of the wind or the barking of a dog to make it live. The only sounds were the chomping of the horse's hooves a little way behind them, and the footsteps of Megan and Roan as they went along the wooded sidewalks.

'I'd love to see inside these houses,' Megan said.

'So you shall.'

She tilted her head to look at him. At five feet and six inches she had always thought of herself as tall, but she found that she had to tilt her head quite far back to see Roan's face—he was a tall man indeed. 'I thought you said everything is locked.'

'I have the key to one of the houses.' At her look of surprise he grinned, the attractive grin that did such amazing things to her heartbeat. 'Influence. Can be a great help sometimes!'

The key belonged to a cottage that stood almost at the end of the street. A narrow cottage with walls that had once been white and were now a weathered grey. The roof was red and sloping and a few stone steps led up to the little stoep with its low wall giving it privacy from the street.

Megan saw Roan's smile as she tiptoed through the door. 'My way of paying homage to history,' she smiled in return as she defended herself.

They walked into the kitchen, a dark room with

creaking floorboards and a lead-paned window that looked out on to the street. The walls were smudged with the dust of the coals that had burned in the great black stone oven. Near the oven was a table with mixing bowls, enormous earthenware bowls that fitted one into another. Megan fingered them, wondering at the woman who had lived here and had used them.

'They're heavy even when they're empty,' she said with respect. 'What strength women must have needed to cope in those days!'

'Would you have liked to live in this house, Megan? You'd have spent your days making soap and churning milk into butter. And for a little light relief you'd have turned to kneading bread.'

She caught the note in his tone, and knew he was teasing. Yet for some reason she allowed her imagination free rein. She had already pictured Roan in this valley, a hard tough prospector. She could see him now in this house, returning home after a frustrating day on the diggings, tired, impatient perhaps, hungry. Somewhere in this picture there had to be a wife, a woman who had a meal ready and waiting, a hot thick soup and a loaf of crusty home-baked bread. A woman who would listen sympathetically to his tales of the day's work, who when the meal was over would use her hands to massage the weariness from his forehead and the strain from his aching back. The woman of her imagination took on features, a face that she recognised. *My* face, Megan realised with sudden shock. And now I really am letting myself be carried away!

Aloud she said, 'I think I'm a little more of a mod-cons girl.'

'Dish-washers and tumble-driers and parties every night?'

'None of those. But soap bought from the super-market, and water that I don't have to heat myself.'

He laughed, the sound low and vital, and doing strange things to an imagination that was already too active for comfort. 'Seems there are no nice old-fashioned girls around any more.'

'Seems not,' she returned, her voice deliberately light to hide the way he was affecting her. 'Let's see the rest of the house.'

Up a narrow rickety staircase they climbed, their footsteps almost deafeningly loud in the silent house.

'Can you picture the women who climbed these stairs in long skirts they could trip on?' Megan asked softly.

'No need to whisper. The only ones who can hear you are the ghosts—and we don't believe in those, do we?' Roan said with amusement.

She hadn't even realised that she was whispering. Yet loud voices in this forsaken house that had once been a home seemed in some way an invasion of privacy. An increased invasion, because of course they were invaders already. Was Roan right about not believing in ghosts? Few girls in today's world would admit to believing in them, yet the musty dimness was a little—well, ghostly, to say the least.

A door creaked eerily on rusty hinges as Roan opened it and preceded Megan into a bedroom. Such a simple room. Tiny, yet functional. A bed with a faded patchwork quilt against one wall, a wooden chair in a corner, and on a dresser a great pitcher and a basin. The woman of the house had had more than just her long skirts to contend with when she had climbed the narrows steps at night.

Above the dresser was a mirror. Megan peered into it. The face that stared back at her from the dusty glass was out of place in the old-fashioned oval wood frame. Honey-coloured hair swinging loose, wide green eyes that were not at all demure, and lips shaded in a clear coral lipstick and uptilted at the corners. The face of a modern girl.

About to step away from the mirror, she saw Roan's face reflected above her own. She had not realised that he had come up behind her, that he was standing quite so close to her.

'The face doesn't fit the mirror,' she told him, a little unsteadily.

'It could.'

The hands that went to her hair took her by surprise, causing her to draw in her breath. She remained quite still as Roan caught up her hair and pushed it into a loose semblance of a bun held fast on the top of her head. In a moment her appearance was changed, suddenly acquiring a touch of the old world. Green eyes widened and found themselves held by brown ones in the mirror, dark eyes that were deep with an enigmatic expression she had not seen in them before. Megan felt her heart beating hard against her chest.

'Quite a difference,' she heard Roan say.

'Quite a difference,' she admitted jerkily. 'All I need now is a crinoline!'

He was so close to her that she could feel the warmth of his body, could sense the hardness of his muscled chest and limbs. Where his arms lay against her neck, the skin burned. On the horse she had been close to him, and she had been acutely aware of him then too, but in a different way.

He laughed softly. 'You look very shapely in jeans, Megan, and that green shirt matches your eyes, did you know?' Again he held her gaze in the mirror. For a long moment there was silence. Roan still held the hair in place above her head, and Megan wondered if he could hear the sound of her heart in the silent room.

And then he had dropped her hair, and as it fell back to her shoulders he was moving away from her. When he said, 'Let's go,' she was glad. There was an atmosphere in this room. They could not have stayed in it longer without something happening. He would have kissed her, she sensed.

Could he have kissed her? Surely not after so short an acquaintance. How long had she known him, in fact? About an hour? It seemed longer.... Of course he could not have kissed her, and she was glad they were leaving the room, the house. Yet as they walked through the creaking front door and out on to the sunny stoep she experienced a stab of self-revelation that told her she was not glad at all.

Thunder stopped his pacing as they came into sight. Roan helped Megan on to the saddle, and this time she put her arms around him without being told. They left the village and emerged into the veld. The air was sweet with the scent of trees and wild flowers, smelling all the sweeter after the mustiness of the house. The horse moved more quickly, and Megan let her arms tighten their hold. She did not want to risk falling, she told herself.

This time there was familiarity in the feel of the hard waist beneath her hands, the hard chest beneath her thumbs. Was it only a few hours since she had waved goodbye to her parents? 'Write to us the moment you get there,' her mother had reminded her in the moments before the train left. 'We want to know everything.'

They would have watched the train vanish from sight, and then they would have driven away in their separate cars, Dad to the office, Mom back to the house on the slope of a Pretoria hill, where the jacarandas were just coming into mauve bloom. Today was Mom's bridge afternoon, she had only just taken up the game again, and while she played her mind would be on Megan. She would be with her in spirit, imagining her arrival at Bronze Mountain, wondering about her reception, and whether she had met Brendon Stevens.

A frown creased Megan's forehead, to be chased away moments later by a smile. How amazed her mother would be to know the way this day had turned out! Megan's luggage at the station. The staff at Bronze Mountain unaware that she had already arrived. The inevitable meeting with Brendon Stevens delayed.

Mentally she began to compose a letter. 'Darling Mom and Dad, have you ever seen a ghost town? I've just walked right through one. No, not Bronze Mountain; that's a resort and will soon be bustling with holidaymakers. This was a real ghost town, the strangest place you ever saw. My luggage is at the station, it will be collected today or tomorrow. I went to the ghost town on a horse. I'm on the horse now, and my arms are around a man who is like nobody I have ever met.'

The smile widened. Mental letters were fun. You could say in them the things you would not put down in writing. 'A tall man,' the letter went on. 'His face is rugged and tanned, and he has laughter lines in all the right places. But there are other lines too, I see them when he looks serious, and I wonder how they got there. Will I ever know him well enough to ask him? His name is Roan, and he has a hard tough body, and just for a moment I wondered what it would be like if he were to kiss me.'

The horse quickened its pace, and Megan had no compunction about letting her arms tighten just a fraction more. 'I love being on this horse, with my arms around this man,' she wrote. 'I have the craziest desire to rest my head against him. Dare I?'

She did dare, she decided. Gently she let her cheeks lie against Roan's back. Very lightly. So lightly that with the speed of the horse and the sigh of the wind he would never notice it.

The scenery grew wilder and more mountainous. Roan seemed to know the veld well. He did not ride by the side of the road but made his way through trackless scrub. Evidently he came here often.

As the horse began to slacken pace, Megan lifted her head quickly. Roan turned in his seat, just far enough so that she could see his profile. It was impassive; he had not felt the cheek against his back. She drew a breath of relief.

'Are you one for views?' he asked her.

'When they're worth seeing.'

'Then you'll love the one I'm about to show you.' As lithely as before he vaulted to the ground and reached out his hands to her, 'Will Ma'am allow me to show her the way?'

'She may consider it.' As Megan responded with a teasing smile to match his own, she made a silent wish that there would be many other things that Roan would show her.

She waited while he tethered the horse to a tree, then she walked beside him along the narrowest of paths. Hardly a path really, more a swathe of flattened brush where others had walked before them. Long grass pricked at Megan's legs through her jeans, and the air was fresh and spiced with the scent of the yellow mimosas that seemed to grow everywhere.

They came to a pile of rock, and Roan held out his hand. Megan could have negotiated the rocks herself, the girl who had once been a tomboy had scrambled over rocks and climbed trees with as much ease as the boys she had played with, but there was something tempting about the proffered hand. She took it and was not surprised that the fingers that closed over hers were warm and firm, giving her pleasure. Roan, it seemed, had given her pleasure from the moment she had met him.

And then they were on soft brush again, but the hand still held hers. Megan made no attempt to pull away. There was something entirely natural in the loose clasp of the two hands, a rightness, and a joy that she was in no hurry to end.

In silence they walked on, and she was acutely aware of the long body so close to her that there were many moments when his leg and his arm touched hers. She wondered what he was thinking.

At the end of a plateau they stopped, and Megan drew in her breath. They were at the edge of a precipice, and in front of them and to all sides stretched a glorious panorama of valleys, and beyond them an escarpment, one mountain folding behind the next as far as the eye could see.

'The Drakensberg?' she asked, looking up at Roan.

'Yes.' His eyes were on the mountains, and in them was an expression that caught at Megan's heart. It was as if he had not been this way in a long while, and was renewing his acquaintance with a sight that meant much to him.

After a few moments he looked down at her. 'Yes, Megan, the Drakensberg. People think of them as being in Natal, but here, in the Eastern Transvaal, is where the escarpment begins.'

'You have a special feeling for mountains, don't you?'

There was a strange expression in the eyes that met hers. It was as if Roan had had a glimpse of something unexpected, a rapport he had not anticipated. Megan found she could not move her eyes from his, and she did not know why the moment seemed quite so precious.

'Mountains *are* special to me.' His voice had deepened. 'They've been standing here for thousands of years, and they'll still be standing here long after we've gone away.' His eyes moved, and Megan expelled a breath she had not known she was holding. 'Mountains give one a sense of perspective.'

You've been hurt, she thought. Badly hurt. And her heart reached out to him. She knew so little of this man, yet she liked him more every second.

'I didn't mean to bore you with my philosophising.' His voice had changed, lightened. 'This was meant to be fun.'

'You haven't bored me. And, Roan, it *is* fun.'

There was a sense of wonder in the eyes that came back to her face. 'I think you mean that,' he said, and once more it was as if he had glimpsed the unexpected.

Why? Megan wondered.

They walked a little farther, keeping close to the edge of the plateau. Roan was still holding her hand, and now she was glad of the security it gave her. The ground was an uneven mass of stones and scrub, and cacti that pricked the unwary. It would be only too easy to slip, and the fall from up here was not to be contemplated. Yet it was a walk Megan would not have wanted to miss. At every turn there were new vistas, one more breathtaking than the next.

'I never dreamed it would be so beautiful,' she said once, when they paused to gaze into the distance.

'I hope others feel the way you do. If so Bronze

Mountain will be a success.' Before she could respond, he added, 'Hungry?'

'A little.'

'More than a little, I'd say. Beauty fills the eye, it does nothing for the stomach.'

Lunch was a meal set high on a mountain slope. 'Another marvellous view,' Megan sighed as she sat down on a white cane chair on the slastoed porch of a small guesthouse. 'Not that I'm surprised. Seems this place has nothing but marvellous scenery.'

Roan laughed. 'First day out, and you're already becoming blasé!'

'Utterly.' She darted him a smile that was provocatively demure, and wondered when last she had felt quite so happy.

The meal was home-cooked. Megan was even hungrier than she had realised. With relish she bit into the boerewors. The long sausage was spicy, evidently made with ingredients with which she was not familiar. The salad was a crisp mixture of lettuce and tiny marble-sized tomatoes and succulent pieces of avacado pear. Dessert was apple pie with fresh cream. Megan thought she would not manage to eat it, and was amazed to find that she did.

'If this is what fresh air does to my appetite I'll be fat in a month!' she groaned.

'Not with your figure,' Roan countered cheerfully, but with an assessing look that was so entirely male that Megan felt warmth come into her cheeks.

The meal had been served by a friendly-faced woman with tight grey curls and a weathered skin, and as they rose to leave she said, 'It's been good to see you, Roan. Been a long time.'

'Good to see you too,' he told her. 'And we'll be back.'

We. The word gave Megan a stab of pleasure. She saw the woman's eyes on her, friendly still but also curious, and she let her own eyes drop beneath her lashes. She felt suddenly vulnerable. We ... was one word really all it took to produce so much joy?

CHAPTER TWO

'I'VE only been away a day,' her mental letter continued, when she was back on the horse with her arms around Roan's waist, and the attractive male scent of him in her nostrils. 'Not even a day. And I feel exhilarated. There's been so much unhappiness these last months. The dreadful thing that happened to Tammy.... Does it seem possible that I can feel suddenly on top of the world? That after just a couple of hours with a man and his horse the whole world seems to have changed?'

But the world *had* changed. *Her* world, at least. And already she knew that nothing would ever be quite the same for her again.

At a vlei Roan reined in once more. The small pond was almost hidden, fringed by a mass of reeds and tall bulrushes. Roan helped Megan down from Thunder's back, and this time he kept his arm around her waist as they walked the short distance to the water. Suddenly he stopped, and motioned to her to remain silent. For a moment she was puzzled, and then, as she followed his pointing finger, she drew in a breath of delight.

Three ducklings, tiny scraps of life with wobbly legs and sparse feathers, were trying out their first unsteady steps. A big brown duck—the mother?—clucked as it watched. And beside the big duck a drama was unfolding. A fourth egg had cracked, and there was movement inside it. Slowly, very slowly, one more tiny duckling was born into the world.

Yet another egg cracked, and another duckling made

its entrance. Busily, proudly, Mother Duck herded her brood together, nudging at them with her beak.

Megan was enchanted. She turned to the man at her side, unaware that she had been smiling for minutes on end and that her eyes were radiant as emeralds; unaware that the man had been watching her rather than the drama of the ducks.

'You knew?' she whispered.

'Yes.'

'You'd been here?'

'Someone told me. And I judged now would be the right time to come. Enjoy the experience, Megan?'

'Need you ask! It was wonderful, Roan. I'll never forget it.' Her eyes went back to the ducks. 'Look! They're going towards the water.'

'Scared they'll drown?' He sounded amused.

'Yes! No, of course not. It took me months to get water-borne. Roan, how do they know what to do?'

'Instinct.'

'Instinct,' she echoed slowly. 'Isn't it strange that animals have it, and humans don't?'

'I think they do. I think we all do. Though sometimes we don't trust it.' His voice was husky all at once. 'Look at me, Megan.'

The change in his tone made her suddenly shy, and she found she couldn't look at him.

'Megan.' His hand reached towards her, the palm was on her throat, a thumb was under her chin, and his fingers were in the hair on the back of her neck. He was turning her head towards him, and she was turning too, of her own volition as much as of his.

'Roan. . . .'

'Megan.' His face was inches from hers. She could just see his eyes, and his breath was warm on her lips.

'Roan, don't. . . .'

'Trust your instinct, Megan.' He was so close to her that his lips brushed her face as he spoke. 'Don't fight it.'

I don't want to fight! I want you to kiss me. And I've never felt this way before, so vulnerable, so filled with longing.

'I won't hurt you,' he whispered.

And then his lips were brushing her forehead, lingering at the corners of her eyes, dancing light kisses on the sensitive area around her mouth. Her eyes were closed, and her body went soft and pliant as his other hand went to her back, drawing her against him. There had been a rightness in their togetherness in the house and on the horse, in the clasp of their hands on the plateau. There was rightness in this.

His mouth came to rest on hers at last, lightly still, as if he did not want to frighten her, but she could feel contained passion in his hands, in his lips, in the tension of his chest and shoulders. She had been kissed before, and not as lightly as this, but never with a sweetness that was so achingly tantalising. It was a sweetness that spread a sensuous warmth through her body, so that she wished the kiss would never end. The hand that had been on her throat moved downwards, and now both arms were holding her, drawing her closer against him, and she was putting up no resistance. On the contrary, her yielding body was arching towards his as her hands moved to his shoulders and curled around his neck.

He drew away from her at last, and she was conscious only of disappointment. 'With instinct like that, Megan, I'm surprised you've never made love before.' He was teasing her, but his voice was a little ragged.

'How do you know that I haven't?'

'There's an innocence about you. But there's also passion, and it's waiting to be roused.'

By you, Roan? Megan wondered.

'Was it instinct that made you stop?' she said with a lightness she was far from feeling.

'Perhaps. I don't want to rush things. I want very much to make love to you, my dear, but only when you're ready for it.' He pushed a hand through the glossy pale hair. 'You're not ready yet, I think.'

'I don't generally even kiss a man on the first date,' she said shakily, and knew that with Roan generalities did not exist.

'Then it's as well I stopped. Because another few minutes and I couldn't have stopped at all.' He drew her to her feet. 'It'll be getting dark soon, time to be making our way to Bronze Mountain. We'll come back here again, Megan.'

Roan's last words made it easy to go back with him to the tethered horse. There were no regrets as they left the vlei. 'We'll come back here,' he had said, and she knew that he'd meant it.

'It's really been the strangest day,' Megan's letter continued as the horse began to move along the track. 'A wonderful day. On the train all I could think of was Tammy and Brendon Stevens, yet I haven't mentioned either of them to Roan. Why not? Perhaps because I didn't want to spoil the day. Darling Mom and Dad, I think I've fallen in love. There—I've said it! I'm in love with a man I haven't known even a day. That was the kind of thing that would happen to Tammy, only with her it was always infatuation, or so I believed. I've never been infatuated. And I never thought love could happen so quickly. But it has. Miraculously, incredibly, it has happened.'

She would never send the letter to her parents. They

would not approve. Would not understand why she had not found a way, *some* way, of going directly to Bronze Mountain. Would not understand how she could have enjoyed the day when she should have been thinking of Tammy.

No, this was one letter she would never send; she knew that. What she did not know was how she had come to compose it, even mentally. 'I'm in love,' were the words she had used. Amazing words for a person who till now had viewed romantic love with slight cynicism and doubt; who had told her sister more than once that love at first sight was only a myth, and a treacherous one at that.

When the resort was finished a brick archway would stand at its entrance bearing the name 'Bronze Mountain' in curving white letters. Now there was just an iron gate standing open at the head of the asphalt drive. Obeying Roan's command, the horse, which had been moving briskly in the chill air of twilight, slackened its pace to a walk. Megan looked around her and saw the place that was to be home for the next weeks. It was a little as she had imagined it from Tammy's letters, only more beautiful. Tammy had mentioned the recreation hall, and the log cabins, and the barbecues on each patio. But in the main Tammy's letters had dealt with people, and she had not mentioned that each cabin was built to look on to the mountains, nor that the resort was perched at the edge of a canyon that was as awesome a sight as anything Megan had seen that day.

'Hey, Roan!' came a shout from a lanky young man with rumpled hair. 'Got a minute?'

The horse slowed its gait even more as Roan responded, 'Can't it wait, Brian?'

'Urgent, Roan—urgent. Where've you been all day?'

'Out. Everything's always urgent with you, Brian.'

'Hey, that's not fair!' A reproachful look. 'Something's gone wrong with the machinery on the dam-site. It'll be dark soon.'

'Okay, be with you in a moment.'

Turning his head sideways, Roan said, 'Brian's right, it really will be dark soon. Mind if I just drop you off at the office?'

'Of course not.'

'It's probably nothing, but I'd better check anyway. See that little brick house, that's the office. I'll be back for you as soon as possible.'

Megan let him help her off the horse, then she made her way to the little brick house he had pointed out to her. The door was open, and she walked in. A man was consulting a map that was pinned to one wall, and at the sound of her footsteps he turned and regarded her curiously. 'May I help you?'

'I'm Megan Westcott.' And as he continued to look puzzled, 'You should have my letter. I wrote and told you I was coming.'

'Westcott?' He shook his head as he went to the desk and ruffled through a sheaf of papers. 'We were expecting a new clerk. Angela Lewis. . . .'

'Then you don't have my letter?' Some of the joy went out of the day as Megan understood that she would have to explain. She drew a breath. 'I'm Tammy's sister. Tammy Grant's sister.'

He stared at her. 'Good heavens!'

Megan did her best to conceal her dismay. 'You didn't know I was coming? Perhaps someone else attended to the correspondence, and. . . .'

'I'd have known,' he interrupted her, and she saw that his face had lost some of its colour. 'We'd all have known. Tammy Grant's sister! My God! But you said your name was . . .?'

'Westcott. Megan Westcott.'

'Larry Anderson.' He held out his hand. 'Miss Westcott, do you mind if I ask you why you're here?'

'To go on where Tammy left off.' Her voice was very quiet.

'The mural?'

'Yes.' He was still staring at her, as if he had seen a ghost, Megan thought, and she said, 'Unless, of course, you have someone else to do it for you now, Mr Anderson?'

'Larry. We don't stand on ceremony here—may I call you Megan? No, Megan, there's nobody else. The wall is just as Tammy left it. After she. . . . What I mean is, we couldn't find any sketches. How could anyone else have taken over?'

'That's what I thought.' Megan took a step towards him. 'That's the way Tammy worked, without sketches. But *I* have a sketch.'

'I don't understand.'

'The design is one we once worked on together. I thought I could finish the job. I don't know who I should be speaking to. . . .'

'Brendon Stevens.'

Megan felt suddenly cold. 'I see.'

Larry was looking at her sympathetically. 'Mr Stevens isn't here today, I believe, but I can tell you that you're a godsend. We didn't know what to do with the wall.

'Mr Stevens might not want me. . . .'

'He will—despite what happened. You see, he. . . .' Larry broke off. 'Why, here he comes now!'

Megan felt her muscles bunch as she waited to face the person who was responsible for her sister's death.

And then she relaxed, for the man who walked into the office was Roan.

'Roan!' she exclaimed happily.

'Nothing urgent after all. Fixed up yet, Megan?'

'Then you two *have* been introduced?' Larry asked in a strange voice.

'Not officially,' Roan grinned. 'We never did get around to a proper introduction, did we, Megan?'

'Perhaps I should introduce you now,' Larry said without expression. 'Roan, this is Megan Westcott. Megan—Brendon Stevens.'

'What!' The word burst from lips that had gone white. On legs that were suddenly as weak as water, Megan stared at the tall rugged-faced man, who was looking back at her puzzled.

She heard Larry say, very deliberately, 'Megan is Tammy Grant's sister.'

For what seemed like hours, but could have been only seconds, they stared at each other. Megan saw her own shock reflected in the eyes of the man she had thought of as Roan. Despite his tan he was suddenly very pale.

'You can't be Brendon Stevens,' she heard herself say.

'I am.' It was said through tight lips.

'If I'd known I wouldn't have. . . .' She stopped, putting a hand to her mouth.

'Spent the day with me?' he finished for her harshly.

Later she would never remember if she nodded. She did know that no words came from her as she stared at him in horror. Mercifully she was spared the need to say anything further. Brendon Stevens—the man she had called Roan—turned on his feet and walked without a word from the office.

'I thought his name was Roan,' she said, feeling stunned.

'It's the name he's known by,' a warm voice said sympathetically. 'You're shaking, Megan. Why don't you sit down?'

Uncomprehendingly she shifted her eyes in his direction. 'I beg your pardon?'

'You've had a shock.'

Shock? The word was utterly inadequate to describe the way she felt. As if her whole world had been shattered. A world which just an hour ago had seemed no less than perfect. She became aware that she was shaking, and she felt very cold.

'Why don't you sit down?' Larry suggested again.

'I'm all right.' She looked at him bewildered. 'What do I do now?'

'Why don't I show you to a cabin?' He consulted a list. 'You could share with Ann Lindsay, at least temporarily.'

'You mean I should stay?'

Larry gave her an assessing look. 'I don't know what happened between you and Roan. I do know you've had a shock.'

'Yes.'

'But nothing else has changed.'

Everything has changed. Don't you understand that?

'The wall still needs finishing,' he pointed out.

'Roan didn't say that.'

'He didn't have a chance,' Larry said reasonably. 'Seems to me he doesn't know why you're here.' He cocked her a half-smile. 'Unless you told him. You really did spend the day together?'

'We did. And no, the subject never came up.' There had been so many other things to talk about.

'Stay then, Megan. At least until you've had time to think about things. Where's your luggage?'

'At the station. Roan said someone would fetch it

tomorrow.' She looked at the man who was being so helpful, and thought she should explain. 'I got off the train, and there was no bus. Roan was there on his horse. It's a bit complicated,' she finished unsteadily.

'Actually, I think I understand.' He put a reassuring hand on her arm. 'Let's go up to the cabin now, Megan. First thing tomorrow morning I'll drive you to the station to collect your luggage.'

'Thank you. The girl I'm to share with—did you say her name was Ann?—you're sure she won't mind?'

'Positive. Tell you what, though, we'll find her on our way to the cabin and let her know what's happening.'

Ann Lindsay was a landscape gardener. Larry and Megan found her planting purple vygies in a rockery. 'Of course you're welcome to share my quarters,' she said, with a smile that endeared her immediately to Megan. 'I won't be going back myself for a while, but you'll find a jar of instant coffee in the grocery cupboard, and a packet of biscuits. Make yourself at home.'

Megan felt a little more at ease as they walked on. She was even able to take in some of what Larry was saying. There were many more people working here now than there would be when the resort was completed, and so cabins which would eventually be for guests were presently being used by some of the staff. Ann's cabin was one of them.

'Have dinner with me tonight,' Larry invited as they came to the door.

Did he not see that she felt torn apart? That inside she was ripped and bleeding. She stopped herself from saying a flat no. Larry was nice, really nice, it was not his fault that she was desolate. 'I'm a little tired, but thank you,' she told him gently.

'Why don't we take a rain-check on dinner?' He grinned, unoffended.

'I'd like that.' She smiled at him gratefully. 'Thanks for helping me, I think I'll go and make myself that cup of coffee now.'

It was pleasant in the cabin. The décor had been chosen with thought to hot summer days, but there was also a fireplace for chill nights. Curtains, carpets and bedspreads were a pretty blend of green and white, with occasional splashes of yellow. In a few months' time tourists would be using the cabin, one family after another, leaving behind them nothing of themselves. But for the present Ann's personality was evident in the horticultural books that lay scattered on a settee, the sunglasses on the coffee-table, the sweater slung over a chair.

There was also a feeling of emptiness. As Megan waited for the kettle to boil, she knew that the emptiness had nothing to do with the cabin. It stemmed from the hollow feeling within herself.

Restlessly she sipped her coffee. She saw the packet of biscuits Ann had mentioned, she opened it, looked inside and closed it again. She was not hungry,

She wondered when Ann would come in. Wondered too what she could do to occupy herself till then. She walked through the cabin, and took in all there was to see in a few minutes.

Going out on to the patio, she stared over the canyon. This morning she had thought each vista more beautiful than the one before, had been stirred by the grandeur and magnificence all around her. Now there was just the terrible feeling of emptiness—and of intense pain. She could not wait here until Ann came, she would go mad if she did.

Larry had pointed out the recreation hall. This was as good a time as any to go and look at the wall. The sooner she saw how much Tammy had accomplished, the sooner she would be able to assess what still had to be done.

There was nobody near the building. Finding the door open, she went inside. She saw the mural immediately. The abstract design covered about a quarter of the side of one wall. Remembering the fun she and Tammy had had when they had planned it, Megan was swept with sorrow. Even now she found it hard to believe that her pretty sister was no longer alive.

Which thought brought her back to Brendon Stevens. To Roan. . . . She curled her nails into her palms so tightly that the skin felt as if it would tear. Stop thinking of Roan! Deliberately she went closer to the wall.

Tammy had done a good job, but there was so much left to do—more than she had imagined. What if Megan decided not to continue with the job after all? It was unlikely that anyone else could complete it. The wall could be painted over, of course, it could be painted the same pale yellow as the other walls. But the beginnings of the mural would be obliterated. What Tammy had left behind her would be gone. It seemed to Megan as if something that remained of the essential Tammy would be gone at the same time.

For her sister's sake she had to complete the mural.

There was nothing she could do until tomorrow. The sketches were in her suitcase. She could not even lay them out on the table in the cabin and study them.

Leaving the recreation hall, Megan looked around her uncertainly. Behind her lay Ann's cabin. There was no sense in going back there just yet. She chose instead to walk along a path that led through the resort. Here and there she passed gardeners and bricklayers, one person called out a greeting and she waved a hand in response.

She did not know where the path would lead her, but when it passed beyond the cabins and went on towards the canyon, she continued to follow it. At the edge of the cliffs, beside some big boulders, the path came to an end, but Megan saw that a narrow hiking trail began just beneath the boulders, snaking its way through the underbrush towards the bottom of the canyon.

The sun was setting now, and the view was breathtaking. The sky was a smudged palette of vermilion and gold, gilding the rugged slopes with a translucent shimmer. Of all the views Megan had seen today, this one was the most spectacular. It was not hard to understand why the spot had been chosen to be the site of the resort.

'Bronze Mountain,' a low voice said from behind her.

Megan spun round. 'Roan!'

'The mountain there on the left, do you see it?' He gestured. 'The sheer rock is all bronze in the twilight.'

She saw it, and another time she would come here again to drink in the beauty more fully. Now she had something else on her mind.

'I didn't hear you come,' she said.

'The path is so sandy that footsteps don't make much sound.'

'Did you follow me, Roan?' She frowned. 'Brendon— I should call you Brendon.'

'Nobody calls me Brendon,' he said briefly.

It was the name at the bottom of the letter. Brendon Stevens. It was also the name that Tammy had used when she'd mentioned him. But Tammy, her sister remembered, had not been one for nicknames.

'You did follow me, didn't you?'

'Of course.'

His face was bleak and hard, and all at once she was frightened. Without thinking she took a step backwards.

A hand reached out and seized her arm, and she was unable to suppress a gasp as her arm went rigid.

'You're frightened.' The hardness had intensified.

'No,' she said jerkily.

'Killing girls by throwing them into canyons isn't my scene.'

An absurd nervousness mingled with excitement at his closeness—she was stirred by him even now, when she knew who he was. 'I'm sure it isn't.'

His jaw tightened, and the lines that she had glimpsed in his face earlier, lines that had given her pause for wonder, deepened. 'A tasteless joke in the circumstances.'

The hand left her arm, and it was easier to breathe. Megan asked, 'Why didn't you tell me who you were?'

'Are you suggesting I was hiding my identity?' He looked taut and strained.

'You said your name was Roan.'

'It's the name I'm known by, I've already told you that. What did you expect, Megan? A formal introduction? Somehow we never did get beyond first names. You were a bit of flotsam stranded at a lonely station, so I took you on to my horse. How the hell was I to know that the name Brendon Stevens would have been cause enough for you to stay in a flea-bag of a hotel till tomorrow?'

'You couldn't know, I suppose,' she said after a moment.

'Besides, Megan Westcott—Larry did say your last name is Westcott? How could I have known you were Tammy's sister? Her name was Grant.'

'My father died when I was a baby, and my mother remarried,' she explained.

'You don't even bear any resemblance to Tammy,' Roan commented.

Another fact she had to acknowledge. Megan had only to close her eyes to see her sister's dark hair and blue eyes, a combination that had made one man after another think himself in love with her. There had been no similarity with Megan's fair hair and green eyes, Roan was not the first to comment on that.

'Tammy was beautiful,' she said slowly.

'Hell, you are too!' he exclaimed. 'That's not what I mean. I'm not just talking about appearances. Even after one day I know that your personality is totally different from your sister's.'

Perceptive man. They *had* been different. Almost the only interest they had shared was their love of art.

But that was not the uppermost thought in Megan's mind. Roan had called her beautiful. For a few moments the blood pulsed in her veins.

And then she reminded herself that but for Roan Tammy would still be alive. A few hours ago she had thought herself in love with Roan. Now she knew that he could mean nothing to her.

'We were different,' she admitted dully.

'Then how the heck. . . .' His words trailed away as he passed a hand before his eyes. It seemed to Megan that he was making a great effort to gain control of his emotions. His shoulders were rigid, and the muscles in his throat were bunched tight. The watching girl felt a wave of pity—an irrational pity, she told herself. She could not let herself feel sorry for Roan. He had killed her sister. Not intentionally, that was obvious, but it had happened, and nothing in the world could erase that terrible fact.

'Is there any point in telling you I'm sorry?' He dropped his hand, and the eyes that met hers were tormented. Pity wrenched inside Megan. 'Do you realise that I'm so sorry it happened?'

Sorry. The word chased the pity, for now she was filled with anger. Sorry indeed! There had been the note—short to the point of terseness. Every word was branded in her memory. 'Dear Mr and Mrs Grant, I want to tell you how much I regret the motor accident in which your daughter Tammy was killed.' There had been more, but not much more. A typewritten letter. Not even the name, Brendon Stevens, had been written by hand.

Perhaps there was not much more he could have written. Perhaps his style of writing was always terse. But he could have come to see them, could have sat down with Mom and Dad and wept with them. Could have. . . .

'I'm sure you're sorry,' she said icily.

She heard the hiss of indrawn breath. As he had done in the office half an hour earlier, she saw him go pale. He looked as taut as if he was on the point of exploding.

Once more Megan felt a wave of pity, then she remembered the note, and she hardened herself against Roan.

'You'd be inhuman if you weren't sorry,' she said.

'You don't believe me.'

'I didn't say that.'

He turned towards the canyon. She couldn't see his face now, but she could see his body—the body that hours earlier had stirred her with its maleness and sexuality. The long muscled legs, the arms that had held her to him in a closeness that had been more wonderful than anything she had ever dreamed possible.

How would she feel if he were to kiss her again? Could the wonder, the magic, be recaptured? She shook

her head, appalled at herself for the thought. Roan
would never kiss her again, she would not let him touch
her again. It would be a betrayal of her sister, of her
parents, if she did so.

He looked so tense, so rigid. What was he thinking?
Was he remembering the accident? He was suffering,
she could see that, but she steeled herself into thinking
that it was right that he should. So little was known
about the accident, but it seemed there had been a
party. Mom and Dad believed that Brendon Stevens
had been drinking. He did not have the appearance of a
drinker, but appearances could be deceiving. Megan
and her parents had had no facts to go on, they had just
speculated. But if Roan had known that his faculties
were impaired he should not have driven. Had he
allowed someone else to drive Tammy and himself
back to Bronze Mountain that night her sister might
still be alive.

The hands at Roan's sides clenched into fists. His
throat muscles grew more bunched, his stance even
more rigid. He had the look of a man who was
struggling with himself, Megan thought. She should
walk away. But something kept her at the edge of the
canyon, her eyes unable to move from Roan.

Abruptly he turned. His lips were still tight, but in his
eyes was a new expression. He looked as if he had
reached a decision. As he opened his mouth to speak
Megan held her breath wondering what was coming.
The words that emerged from his lips were so mundane
that she knew she had let her imagination run wild.

'I'll drive you to the station tomorrow.'

'Thank you, but. . . .'

'We'll fetch your luggage.'

Didn't he realise that she could not sit in a car with
him?

'Larry has offered already,' she told him, keeping her voice light.

'I didn't take you for the slick type, Megan.' His voice was harsh.

'I'm not.'

'Then why don't you come straight out with it and say that you can't trust yourself in a car with me?'

Megan felt her heart pounding against her ribs. Remorse-stricken Roan might be, but even now he had lost none of his strength and maleness. On the contrary, there was something very fierce about him at this moment.

'You're being overly dramatic.' She forced a casual note.

'Am I?' he asked very quietly. 'Would you let yourself be driven by the man who drove the car in which your sister met her death?'

She stared at him, unable to answer, knowing what to say, yet unable to say it.

Without warning he stepped forward and grasped her shoulders in his hands. 'Am I being over-dramatic?' he demanded.

The last time his hands had touched her there had been warmth in the fingers, and sensuousness. Sensuousness above all else. And she had responded— as she was responding again, although there was no warmth now, just a cruel insistence that she speak.

She moistened her lips. 'I told you—I've arranged with Larry. . . .'

He made an impatient sound in his throat. 'All right then, have dinner with me tonight.'

His fingers were biting into her shoulders. 'You're hurting me,' she said in a choked tone.

The grip relaxed, but the hands remained where they were, and through the turmoil of her thoughts she was aware of every long finger.

'Will you have dinner with me, Megan?'

'I can't, I'm sorry.'

'Because I'm Brendon Stevens?'

She was trembling. 'Because I'm tired.'

An eyebrow rose. You didn't seem tired earlier. By the vlei, when you responded to my kisses, you were anything but tired.'

Her cheeks warmed, but she did not attempt to deny the statement. She had been in love and exhilarated. Even now she was stirred by him, this dynamic man with the rugged face and lithe body and compelling eyes. She had never met anyone like him. She had also never met a person who showed quite so little compunction for his deeds. Motor accidents happened, they happened every day. What had made Brendon Stevens a monster in the eyes of Megan and her parents had been the almost complete lack of remorse he had shown in the matter.

'Perhaps a few kisses would revive you.'

She had not known he could be so mocking. In the long hours she had spent with him she had seen only one side of the man, and in her naïveté she had thought she knew him. Now she was seeing another aspect of Roan, one she did not like at all, and she was suddenly very angry.

'Don't touch me!' she hissed.

'You weren't averse to it the first time. Correct me if I'm wrong, but you seemed to enjoy it.'

'That was before I knew who you were.' The words were out before she could stop them.

She heard the sound he made in his throat as he moved closer towards her and his hands tightened on her shoulders once more, the fingers biting into them. Her senses leaped, as much with excitement as with fear. She managed to take a step away from him.

'You *are* frightened of me.' There was hardness in the rugged face, bitterness in the lines around the sensuous lips and in the dark eyes.

'No.' She tried to conceal the turmoil churning inside her.

'Well then?' he persisted, as his fingers maintained their ruthless grip.

'You know the score as well as I do.'

'I know that I drove the car in which your sister died.' His mouth twisted, with pain she thought. 'I also know that we had a good thing starting for us, Megan.'

A wonderful thing. Magical. Too magical. A fairy story in which the prince had become the demon.

'It's impossible,' she said simply. 'You must see that.'

'Do you want me to spend the rest of my life atoning for what happened?' His face was a rigid mask.

'Of course not.'

'I told you how sorry I was. I told your parents.'

'You wrote, yes.' She forbore to say how curt and unfeeling the note had been. 'Why didn't you come to see us?'

Dark eyes grew hooded, and he seemed to hesitate a moment before saying, 'It wasn't possible.'

'You couldn't spare the time, I suppose,' she flung at him.

He looked down at her, and the expression in his eyes suggested an emotion which Megan did not understand. She had thrown him a challenge. How would he deal with it?

He looked down at her for what seemed a long time, interminable. Her breathing grew jerky as she waited for his response. She was not aware that he was still holding her shoulders until she felt them being released, and saw his hands fall to his sides.

'There's no point in continuing with this discussion,' he said flatly.

To Megan, whose nerves were stretched to breaking point, the quietly-spoken words were almost an anticlimax.

Abruptly he stepped away from her. 'Roan!' The name emerged without volition. The object of the plea—was it a plea?—gave no indication of hearing her as he strode away. Megan watched him go, tall and lithe and powerful, the confident gait showing none of the pain and uncertainty which had surfaced for a minute or two. She watched him merge with the trees and shrubs of the darkening veld. Only when he was out of sight did she put her hands over her eyes and let a strangled sob escape from her throat.

CHAPTER THREE

IT was with a sense of depression that she made her way back to the cottage. A light was on, and when she came into the kitchen she found Ann switching on the kettle.

'Hello, I wondered where you were, you're just in time for some coffee.'

'Lovely,' Megan said gratefully.

'Been exploring?'

'... Yes.'

Ann looked at her so perceptively for a moment that Megan wondered whether she had caught the unhappiness in her tone. If Ann were to ask where she had been, what she had seen, it was doubtful that she could answer with any degree of control. To change the subject she said, 'Tell me what I can do to help.'

'You could get out the cups. The toaster too, I'm going to have a slice of toast, a sort of pre-supper snack, will you have one too?'

There was something extremely appealing about Ann, Megan decided. She liked the openness of her smile and the laughing warmth in her eyes.

They sat down with toast and coffee at a round wooden kitchen table. Megan took a sip of the coffee and felt the hot liquid warm her throat, a warmth that spread to her arms, where Roan had touched them, to her fingers. She had not realised how cold she was.

'I didn't know you were Tammy Grant's sister,' Ann observed.

'Neither did Roan.' The words were out before she could stop them.

'So you've met.' Compassion warmed the other girl's eyes.

'This morning. We spent the day together.' There was something about Ann that made it easy to speak. 'I didn't know he was Brendon Stevens.'

'Would it have made any difference if you had?'

I wouldn't have experienced the most wonderful day of my life. Nor the shock and the turmoil with which it ended.

After a moment, when Megan had not answered, Ann went on, 'I have a feeling you met him again, while you were exploring.'

Megan's head jerked up. 'How did you know?'

'You looked very white when you came in a few minutes ago, and I wondered why.'

'We met.' Megan's voice was low.

'Want to talk about it?'

If ever the time came when Megan needed a confidant, Ann would be that person. But she was not yet ready to talk. There were emotions which she had to understand, had to come to terms with. Until then she could not talk about Roan and what had happened to Tammy.

She shook her head. 'I don't think so.'

'That's okay. I just want to say one thing, Megan, don't judge Roan too harshly.'

If only I could judge him impartially, Megan thought. I fell in love with Roan. Just now, in the sunset, even knowing who he was and what he had done, I could feel myself responding to him. At this moment I'm so uncertain of myself that I don't know whether I'm judging him too harshly or not harshly enough.

Ann broke the silence that had fallen between them.

'Larry tells me that you've come here to finish the mural.'

'It was my intention.'

Ann looked at her curiously. 'The way you say that sounds as if you might have changed your mind.'

Megan met her eyes. 'I'm no longer sure.'

'Roan has given you cause to doubt?'

Megan hesitated, then she said, honestly, 'Yes.'

'You must have known he'd be here.'

I knew there would be a Brendon Stevens, and I thought I would deal with him. In fact I looked forward to telling him what I thought of him. What I didn't know was that there would be a Roan, and that I would fall in love with him.

'Sometimes,' she said lightly, 'an imaginary situation turns out to be very different from reality.'

Ann's eyes were thoughtful, as if she was wondering what it was that had happened between Roan and Megan. At last she said, 'Tammy was in the midst of something wonderful.'

'I know, I saw it.'

'But she left no sketches. After ... after she died ... we searched through her things, but we found nothing.'

'It was all in her head. That was the way Tammy worked,' Megan explained.

'But you feel able to complete the mural?'

It would be so easy to say no. An easy escape.

'I have the sketches.' Megan spoke slowly, painfully. 'We worked on them together before Tammy came to Bronze Mountain.'

Ann'e eyes sparkled. 'You're an artist too, then?'

'I do art-work for an advertising company. I had three weeks' leave due to me, and I decided to come here and work on the mural. I asked for a few additional weeks' leave.' She made a rueful mouth. 'A crazy impulse.'

'A wonderful impulse!' More gently, Ann said, 'Don't go away, Megan.'

'The wall could be painted over.'

'No.'

'Another artist could be brought in. Someone with new ideas.'

'Who would destroy Tammy's memory?' Ann's tone was quiet.

Megan bit her lip. 'I'd thought of that.'

'Well then?'

Megan was silent a long moment. Ann's eyes were on her, steady and compassionate. It was obvious the other girl knew her reluctance concerned Roan, equally obvious that she did not understand it, for Megan had known that she would meet Brendon Stevens at Bronze Mountain.

'I'll do it,' she said at length, shakily.

'I'm so glad!' Ann's voice was warm with delight. 'Another piece of toast?'

'No, thanks.'

'Had you thought about supper?'

Megan looked up. 'No.'

'People do pretty much as they like here. There's a shop in the complex, when the resort is ready the guests will buy their supplies there. It's open already, the staff buy there at a discount.'

'And you do your cooking here.' Megan gestured to the stove.

'Right. Sometimes a few of us get together for a braaivleis. There's a cafeteria near the gate, and a few miles down the road there's a restaurant.'

'Quite a choice,' Megan commented.

'Had I known you were coming I'd have suggested

we grill some steak outside—the weather's ideal for a braaivleis—but as it is I've already agreed to a date.'

'Don't worry about me.' Megan's quick smile hid her disappointment. She was not hungry, but she would have enjoyed Ann's company. 'I'll manage.'

'Help yourself to whatever you can find, tomorrow we'll work out some sort of system.'

'You're very kind.'

'Not at all. I know what it's like to be new somewhere.' Ann glanced at her watch. 'Heavens, just look at the time! I have exactly five minutes to shower and change.'

The cabin seemed empty again when Ann had gone— too quiet. Restlessly Megan leafed through a magazine, only to put it back on the pile. The evening stretched ahead of her and she did not know what to do with herself. Pity the sketches were with her luggage at the station, she could have studied them with a thought to what had already been done.

A knock at the door had her starting up in alarm. Was it Roan? What would she say to him? But the man who stood smiling at her as she opened the door was Larry, and he was holding some towels.

'Thought I'd drop these,' he said cheerfully. 'Bet Ann didn't have time to think of them herself.'

'Thank you.' Megan smiled back at him. 'I didn't think of them either.'

'Ann gone out?'

'Yes.'

'And you've had no supper.'

'We did have toast and tea together.'

'Call that decent food?' Larry rolled his eyes. 'Do you feel any drops, Megan?'

'Drops?' She looked at him uncomprehendingly.

'Raindrops.'

'Why, no. There isn't even a cloud in the sky. It couldn't be. . . .' She stopped as she saw that he was laughing. 'You're joking!'

'Not altogether. We said we'd take a rain-check on our dinner together. You're all alone here, why don't you change your mind and have dinner with me tonight?'

Megan looked at him. He was young, at least six years younger than Roan, who looked to be about thirty-four. His fair hair was rumpled and his smile was boyish. There was something very likeable about Larry.

It had been a shattering day in more than one respect, and the thought of a lonely evening in the cabin was depressing. She wasn't hungry, but the prospect of a few hours in this very nice young man's company was all at once appealing. With a sudden lifting of her spirits she smiled back at him.

'You'll change your mind?'

'That's a girl's prerogative, isn't it?' She threw him a smile. 'I don't have any pretty clothes with me right now.'

A glance that was thoroughly male swept over her, both assessingly and approvingly. 'You look very nice just as you are. Out here people tend to wear whatever makes them feel comfortable.'

'I'm glad,' she said, and knew that she really was glad at the thought of leaving the oppressive stillness of the cabin. 'Thanks for the towels, Larry. I'd like to take a shower before we go. Ten minutes suit you?'

The restaurant was panelled in knotted wood, and the walls were hung with the memorabilia of the days when the district had been populated with gold-prospectors and their hangers-on. There were photographs of stern-looking men in rough leather jackets and wide-brimmed hats and women in long full skirts. The décor included the utensils of a past era, copper cooking-pots and blackened fire-tongs and a crooked weaving frame.

Above her head Megan saw a picture of a hotel with men in discussion beside their tethered horses on the street outside.

'Pilgrim's Rest,' Larry said.

'I thought as much,' Megan murmured, and tried to suppress a wave of pain. The hotel was almost identical in appearance to the one she had seen in the ghost village.

'I'll have to take you there one day soon.'

Resolutely she turned her eyes away from the picture and smiled at her companion. 'I'm going to be really busy,' she heard herself saying. 'I can only stay here a few weeks, and I have to finish the mural in that time.'

'Even busy ladies take time off occasionally. Tammy seemed to be one for the bright lights.'

She did not want to discuss her sister, just as she did not want to visit Pilgrim's Rest—both would worsen wounds that were already too raw.

'Tammy enjoyed life,' she agreed lightly, omitting to mention the fact that she and her sister had had very different personalities. 'Just look at those iron picks, Larry. They must weigh a ton! Can you imagine that people actually worked with them?'

The ploy worked, for Larry was content to change the subject. By the time the waitress came to take their order they were discussing a movie each had seen recently.

In a few months' time the restaurant would be crowded with tourists, but now it was filled with the people who worked at Bronze Mountain. Larry seemed to know everyone, he was constantly responding to waves or smiles. A resort in the process of construction would be a little like a small village, Megan reflected. Everyone would know everyone else, their strengths and their weaknesses; their secrets. There would be the same lack of privacy, what one person did would be known to all. There would be talk.

What talk had there been about Tammy and Roan? What was the relationship that had existed between them? All she knew was that there had been a party, and that the accident had happened on the way back. What *had* there been between Tammy and Brendon? Tammy and Roan?

She should have been prepared for the emotion that hit her, like a blow, in the area around her ribs. Tammy and Roan, together. The mental picture hurt.

In an effort to change the gist of her thoughts, she turned her eyes to the dance-floor where a three-piece band was beginning to play. The musicians were bearded, and their rough clothes were similar to those worn by the prospectors in the photographs. 'Even the band is in keeping with the décor,' she remarked, when she felt her emotions were sufficiently under control to make it safe to look back at her companion.

'The music too—the tickey-draai and *Jan Pierewit*.' Larry laughed, as he cocked his head to the well-loved folk-tunes. 'Fortunately they won't keep this up. When they change to disco stuff we'll dance. Meawhile, have you decided what you'd like to eat?'

Actually she didn't feel like eating at all. But the waitress, in the long dress of a prospector's wife, was taking orders at a neighbouring table. Megan forced herself to concentrate on the menu.

Larry gave their order and presently the music changed, and they got up to dance. Larry made a light attempt to hold her close, but when Megan gave him to understand that it was not what she wanted he did not persist. He really was nice, she thought gratefully, amusing and generous and sensitive enough to respect her feelings.

She was just beginning to relax against him when Roan walked in, a pretty blonde girl at his side. In an instant Megan went rigid. Larry must have sensed her reaction, for he turned his head in the direction she was looking, and then, with a sudden lack of his former gentleness, he pulled her tight against him.

Roan had seen her in the moment that she had seen him. Across the room he coolly met her appalled gaze. If he was as shocked as she was, he did not show it. There was just a thinning of lips that looked suddenly cruel, and a cynical lift of one eyebrow. Megan raised the hand that rested on Larry's shoulder in a tiny gesture of appeal, but it was lost on Roan. Inclining his head towards his companion, he said something and smiled as he put his hand on her waist and led her to a table.

'Relax, honey.' Larry was holding her so close that his breath fanned her ear, but his voice seemed to come from afar.

Relax? Her stomach muscles were taut and her head was pounding. She should have realised that she might see Roan here tonight, there could be very few places of entertainment in the area. She should have been prepared. Why hadn't she been?

'Relax,' Larry said again. His hands were on her back now, touching her with a familiarity she did not like.

She managed a smile. 'I'm relaxed.'

'You were until Roan walked in.'

'I still am.' On the periphery of her vision she saw rescue in the form of the waitress who was putting a tray on their table. 'I see our meal has arrived. I'm starving, Larry, why don't we eat before the food gets cold?'

She wasn't starving at all. She was not even remotely hungry. But she pushed the food determinedly around on her plate, and forced herself to eat. Anything else would have drawn comment from Larry; it would also, in the circumstances, have been discourteous.

She tried not to look in the direction of the dance-floor where Roan was dancing with the blonde girl. But now and then her eyes were drawn that way, almost against her will it seemed, and the sight of the two dancing close together was torment.

'Her name is Petra,' Larry said.

Megan looked at him blankly, wondering what had gone before. She knew that she had taken in only fragments of his conversation. 'Petra?' she repeated tentatively.

'Roan's girl-friend.'

Megan flinched. Had Larry used the word 'girl-friend' deliberately when he could have said, 'the girl Roan is dancing with' instead? She looked up and saw that he was smiling at her, the boyish smile that had endeared itself to her earlier. Strangely, the smile did not reach his eyes.

'Really?' she responded lightly.

'Petra's work deals with recreational planning. A few of the guys have been after her, but it seems she fancies Roan.'

'He's an attractive man.' Still spoken with lightness. She did not know why Larry was baiting her, for it was obvious that this was what he was doing. Her momentary tension on the dance-floor was surely not reason enough.

'Talking about recreation,' she changed the subject,

'tell me what's planned for Bronze Mountain. Will there be tennis courts and a pool?'

'And a golf course,' he told her, and she was glad to see his returning enthusiasm.

They talked and ate, and Megan was astonished to discover that she was capable of awareness on two levels at the same time. She was able to carry on a conversation with Larry, when all the time she was aware of Roan. She did not even have to look at the dance-floor to know when he and Petra left it to go back to their table. She was aware of the way in which they talked and laughed together. She knew when Petra picked up her bag and walked in the direction of the washrooms.

And she was aware of the precise moment when Roan stood up. Even before he left his seat she knew which way he would walk. And she felt a sudden chill on her skin and a dryness in her throat.

'Will you dance with me, Megan?' He looked very tall as he stood beside their table. Tall, in command of himself, and dangerously attractive.

'She's here with me,' Larry protested, before Megan could speak.

'I'm merely inviting her to dance.'

'Megan is with me,' Larry sounded sullen. 'You have some nerve, Stevens!'

'When *I* ask a girl to dance it's a nerve,' Roan observed politely. 'I seem to recall seeing you do the same thing.'

Megan saw the angry flush that came into Larry's face, the mutinous set of his mouth. She sensed rather than saw that his hands had balled into fists. Then she darted a look at Roan and saw that his own composure had not been affected.

'Well, Megan?' Roan's eyes, dark and unreadable,

had gone from Larry to her. 'Are you turning me down?'

She knew what she had to do, and she had to do it in such a way that the tension at the table would not become explosive. She had noticed the spirit of easy camaraderie in this restaurant where there were no strangers. On the surface at least, Roan's invitation was not out of line. Smiling up at him, she said, 'I never turn down an invitation to dance, especially when it comes from a man who gave me an enjoyable day.' Another smile was thrown Larry's way, concealing her dismay at his obvious displeasure. 'Don't eat my dessert when it comes—I love strawberries and cream.'

'And do you love Larry as well?' came the question, as Megan moved into Roan's arms.

How can I, when I'm in love with you? Because I *am* in love with you, despite the fact that every rational cell in my brain tells me it's impossible.

'Is that what you think?' she countered.

'On the subject of Larry and females I've learned not to form opinions.'

So she had not imagined the tension between the two men. Strange that Tammy had never mentioned it, but then there were many things that her sister had omitted to mention. Megan was about to tell Roan that Larry meant nothing to her when he went on, and now his voice was hard, 'You seem to have recovered from your fatigue very quickly.'

'I do feel more rested.'

'Or perhaps'—his voice was laced with contempt—'you weren't tired to begin with.'

'Roan. . . .'

'Letting a man called Roan kiss you was a very different thing from going to dinner with a man called Brendon Stevens.'

She shook her head hopelessly. 'You must realise that knowing who you are changes things.'

'Certain things don't change,' he said, so softly that her eyes flicked up to his, green and wide and questioning.

'I don't understand. . . .'

'This afternoon I wanted to make love to you. I want it still.'

Her heart thudded in her chest. 'No, Roan, no!'

'Don't make a scene,' he whispered, as he pulled her closer. 'There are many bored spectators who would give everything for some gossip.'

There was no escaping as he pulled her against him, and in a moment she had to admit to herself that she was in the arms of an expert. To the bored spectators there would be nothing out of the ordinary in the sight of the two people on the dance-floor. They could not know of the deliberate thrust of hard thighs against hers, or the hand that moved with tantalising sensuousness on her back. Megan knew she had never been quite so aware of a man as she was now, had never been so conscious of intimacy. Larry had held her more tightly than Roan did, but her senses had not leaped as they did now, if anything she had felt repulsed. She should be repulsed now, she told herself, but to her shame she could feel only delight, a delight that drowned her anger as it coursed through her body. It was an emotion that was so intense that she had to restrain herself from pressing herself even closer against Roan.

'Enjoying it?' he whispered against her ear.

'No!' she lied.

She heard the hissing intake of breath, and then the movement of the thighs became even more outrageous, and they were dancing as if they were one person, and all of Megan's nerve-endings burned as if they had been set aflame by a thousand searing matches.

The music ended. Roan held her to him a moment longer than was necessary. Then, as the next tune began, he put her from him. Megan stared up at him confused, and saw that his eyes were narrowed, and as intent as if he could see through her clothes, through the outer layers of skin to the turmoil in her soul.

'Petra's back,' she heard him say. 'I'll take you back to your table.'

She found her voice. 'I'll take myself.' Her lips were stiff as she made to move away from him.

A hand took her wrist. 'Thanks for the dance,' he said pleasantly.

'Damn you, Roan!' she countered, almost beneath her breath, and wondered if he had heard her.

The remainder of the evening passed in a blur. Megan ate strawberries and cream that could well have been painted on cardboard, she danced with Larry, and saw Roan dancing with Petra. And none of it meant anything to her.

When it was time to leave the restaurant she wondered if Larry was as relieved as she was to end the evening. She had been a poor companion, she realised remorsefully, looking up at the fair-haired man. She had tried to be vivacious, but he would have been insensitive if he had not seen through the act. She wanted to apologise and could not, because that would have meant explaining how she felt about Roan—and how could she do that when her feelings were so complex that she did not quite understand them herself?

Larry fetched Megan's luggage the next day. She drove with him to the station, and if the stationmaster was surprised to see Larry and not Roan, he made no comment. It was good to have her things, to be able to change into a fresh pair of jeans and a blouse. It was good, too, to be able to get to work. She had come to Bronze Mountain to complete the mural which her sister had begun, and she wanted to get on with it.

After the turmoil she had experienced in the restaurant, Megan had imagined that she would find it difficult to work, that she would be unable to turn her concentration to the intricacies of painting when her thoughts kept turning to Roan. She dreamed of him at night, dreams she was powerless to control. But her daily contact with him was limited. She saw him sometimes—given the smallness of the Bronze Mountain resort it would have been impossible not to—but watching out for him became habit after a while, and she became adept at avoiding him.

However much she thought about Roan, she was nevertheless able to work. Megan's training had been in commercial art. At the advertising agency where she worked her layouts were considered unusual and artistic, and nothing gave her more pleasure than to come up with a new and creative idea. She had also illustrated a book for children, a particularly happy experience. This was the first time she had worked on a mural, and she knew that if only she could stop herself thinking of Roan it too would be a memorable experience.

It was a while since she and Tammy had worked on the sketches. Only recently, when she had been able to bring herself to take them from a drawer and look at them, had she recalled the basic design. Seeing the actual wall and the work Tammy had done on it, Megan realised how closely her sister had kept to the original idea. There were changes, yes, but they were minor ones, the actual theme was the same one that they had devised together so many months ago.

Months. . . . Another time, it seemed to her now. A time when she had still had a sister, temperamental and a little flighty, but funny and warm and loving. A time when there had been no Brendon Stevens in Tammy's life, for Megan did not think her sister had met him then. A time when there had been no Roan.

Stop thinking about Roan, she told herself, more than once, turning her attention to the wall with new vigour.

The weeks would pass, she knew, and the time would come when she would leave Bronze Mountain and go back to her own life. Back to the advertising agency, and the house on the jacaranda-covered hill. There would be Henry, dear Henry who had asked her twice to marry him. Henry was kind and solid and dependable, but she didn't love him. 'The kind of love you're looking for doesn't exist,' her mother had said in exasperation. 'Megan darling, Henry is so nice.' He *was* nice. He was also—the word that came disloyally to mind was 'stodgy'.

Sadly Megan acknowledged that when she saw Henry again he would seem even stodgier than before. So would the other men she knew and dated. 'That's what you've done to me, Roan,' she whispered silently. 'You made me fall in love with you, you've spoiled every other man in the world for me.'

Sometimes she thought she should have stayed in Pretoria. She would never have met Roan. Instead she would have taken a three-week holiday at the coast with a group of friends. True, the mural would never have been finished, but her own peace of mind would have remained intact.

And then she would look at the wall, and try to

visualise it without the partly-finished design. White, blank. Sterile. In time, probably, adorned with a completely different mural, designed and painted by someone else, the warmth and fun which were a part of Tammy and which were reflected in the design no longer even a memory. Painfully she would acknowledge that she *had* been right to come to Bronze Mountain, that to leave here without completing the mural would be to betray her sister.

Life began to slip into a routine. Work on the wall until midday, and then a return to the cabin. Ann would come in from the gardens, and they would do a 'clean-up job' as they laughingly called it. Ann would scrub the mud from her hands, Megan the paint. Then they would prepare lunch, and over bread and a selection of cheese and fruit they would talk. With each day Ann endeared herself more to Megan. There was something warm and open and sympathetic about the other girl. Ann was becoming a good friend.

Lunch over, it was back to the recreation hall until the daylight began to fade, making work impossible. 'You're driving yourself,' Ann told Megan once.

'It's a big wall,' Megan pointed out.

'And you have six weeks to do it in. A few days more or less won't make a difference.'

You don't understand. It makes all the difference in the world. The sooner I finish the mural, the sooner I can leave Bronze Mountain. The sooner I can rid myself of the dread of seeing Roan at every turn of the path.

'Something's worrying you,' Ann observed shrewdly.

'No.'

'The mural?'

'It's going rather splendidly.'

'You'd rather I didn't pry.'

'You're not prying,' Megan protested. 'Mm, doesn't that lettuce look crisp!'

'A change of subject if ever I saw one. I had to pay dearly for that lettuce, Megan, so savour each mouthful—and remember that if ever you do want to talk I'll be around.'

Twice in the first week Larry invited Megan to dine with him, and though she knew the evenings would give her no particular pleasure, she accepted the invitations. It was no fun to spend the hours alone in the cabin when Ann was out. Besides, Megan knew it was important not to forgo the company of other men. I can't remain faithful to a man who's not mine to begin with, she told herself ruefully.

Work, it seemed, came to a near standstill at weekends. Ann was going to spend the two days with her parents in near-by Sabie. Larry invited Megan to go picnicking with him, but she declined. It was one thing to spend an evening with him, an entire day might be too much. The lovely day with Roan was still too raw in her memory. Better by far to be alone.

But she thought of Roan, and the hours they had spent together; she remembered the vlei and the ducklings. All at once she knew what she would do. There were horses at Bronze Mountain, she would take one, and she would ride to the vlei, taking with her a book and a packet of sandwiches.

'It's easy to find,' said Ann, when Megan asked her the way. 'But it's a lonely trail. Why not ask Larry to go with you?'

'I'd rather go alone.'

'Fair enough. I didn't know you'd visited the vlei.'

Megan found herself colouring. 'Roan took me there, that first day. . . .'

Ann looked at her thoughtfully. 'I'm not sure you

should go that way alone,' she said after a moment, quietly. 'But I'll draw you a map if you really want it.'

The sky was blue and cloudless. A slight breeze brushed through the long wild grass and the trees and shrubs that grew everywhere. The stableman had expressed some concern at the fact that Megan intended to ride alone, but she had reassured him—it was not the first time she had been on a horse and she could take care of herself.

The motion of the horse was rhythmic, and relaxing in a way that the ride with Roan had not been, for then Megan had been aware only of sensuousness and the excitement of falling crazily in love. The air was warm and the perfume of wild flowers was pleasant. As she felt tension draining from her, draining from legs and arms and a neck that had been uncomfortably stiff, she understood for the first time just how taut her nerves had been since the disclosure of Roan's identity. It had been a good idea to spend the day away from Bronze Mountain. To be quite alone.

With the help of Ann's map it was not difficult to find the vlei, though if Megan had not recognised the clump of willows that clustered around it she might have ridden right past it. Dismounting, she tethered the horse loosely to a tree and made her way to the edge of the water.

Even in a week the ducklings had grown. Small scraps of fluff, they pecked at seeds in the grass, while the mother duck hovered about them protectively. At Megan's approach there was a shrill squawking, and then mother and babies waddled waterwards. Megan watched entranced, a smile playing around her lips.

'Difficult to believe that just a week ago they were still in their eggs,' a voice observed.

CHAPTER FOUR

HEART thudding against her ribs, Megan forced herself to look around very slowly. 'Very difficult,' she responded, when she could trust herself to speak. 'I didn't hear you come, Roan.'

'You were absorbed in the ducks.'

'Did you follow me?'

'Anyone could have come upon you here.'

'*Did* you?'

'Yes,' he said deliberately, 'of course I did.'

Her heart beat even faster. 'That's the second time you've followed me. I didn't notice you when I left Bronze Mountain. Did you purposely keep your distance so that I wouldn't know you were behind me?'

'Don't be silly.' There was contempt in his tone. 'The stableman was concerned. He told me you'd gone out alone.'

'He had no right to!'

'He had every right, he has a damn sight more sense than you do.'

She lifted her chin. 'Nothing would have happened to me.'

'Alone in the veld? You're naïve, Megan. And as irresponsible as your sister.'

'Leave Tammy out of this!' Her voice shook.

'You're right—I shouldn't have mentioned her.' There was a tightening of the skin around Roan's cheekbones, and in his eyes there was an expression that tugged, quite unexpectedly, at Megan's heartstrings. A haunted expression, she thought, giving it a name, and

65

wondered if she was being fanciful.

Slowly, as if he was willing himself to relax, the tautness lessened. 'Why did you come here?' he asked at last, evenly.

'I wanted to see the ducklings. Wanted to see if they'd grown.'

'Didn't it occur to you that it isn't the wisest thing in the world for a girl to go riding in the veld by herself?'

'Nothing happened,' she said defensively.

'That doesn't make it right. You should have asked someone to go with you.'

'Ann went home for the weekend.'

'And the gallant Larry?'

There was something in his voice that indicated his dislike of the younger man. A dislike that was mutual, she realised, remembering Larry's attitude towards Roan.

'Larry had picnic plans,' she said lightly. 'A group was going to one of the waterfalls.'

'You were invited to join them?'

'Yes.' She met his eyes, and wished she did not feel the need for defensiveness. 'I told you, I wanted to see the ducklings.'

'You could have asked me to ride with you.'

She remained silent.

'But of course you wouldn't do that.' His voice had roughened. 'The last thing you'd want is my company, isn't that so, Megan?'

It's what I want *most*. I love you, Roan. I'm crazy, and it's against all reason, but I can't seem to help myself.

'Don't bother to explain,' he countered harshly, before she could answer. 'We both know how you feel about spending even a moment with Brendon Stevens.'

'That isn't true.' Her head was pounding.

'No? Do you think I'm blind? Do you think I haven't seen the way you change direction whenever you see me come near? Anyway, that's by the way. For today you're stuck with me.'

Her lips were dry. 'Today?'

'Till we get back to Bronze Mountain. It's enough that one sister died—I won't have it said that the other one also came to harm because I was negligent.'

'Then you admit that you were negligent. That....' The words trailed away as his hand seized her wrist, and she felt the colour drain from her cheeks.

'Don't say that.' His eyes were bleak.

'Isn't it true?'

The hand on her wrist tightened, fingers biting into the soft skin. 'You don't know when to stop, do you?'

'I think,' she said recklessly, 'that you don't really give a damn about my safety. It's only your reputation that matters to you.'

She had the satisfaction of seeing the angry sparkle that flickered in his eyes. Then he smiled, deliberately, and without humour. 'You're quite right.'

'You don't care about me at all.'

She didn't know what had made her say the last words. She did know that she regretted them, for the mirthless smile deepened, bringing her pain as he said, 'You don't really want an answer to that question.'

'No, because it's unnecessary.' She smiled back at him, hoping that she was successful in concealing her agitation. 'You can go back now, Roan.'

'You're ready to go, then?'

'I'm staying here.'

He shrugged before taking a few steps away from her, towards his horse, and Megan told herself she was pleased. And then she saw that he was taking an orange from a saddlebag, and a pulse began to beat in her temple.

Roan crouched down on the ground beside her and began to peel the orange, drawing away the skin with easy fingers. Fingers that had once given her pleasure when they had caressed her body. Tautly she watched him.

'Want some?' He looked up at her.

'No. What are you doing, Roan?'

He grinned. 'Isn't it obvious?'

'I told you to go.'

'I don't take well to orders.'

'But you like to give them,' she said.

A strange expression passed before his eyes. Haunted was the word that had come a few minutes earlier to Megan's mind. He dropped his eyes to the fruit, and the expression was concealed.

Feeling tenser than ever, she walked a little away from him and turned her eyes to the ducklings. Tiny balls of fluff, minutes ago she had thought them adorable, but now she had trouble focusing on them. It was hard to focus on anything when all the time she was aware only of Roan.

She should have taken Larry up on his invitation. If the idea of a day in his company had not been especially appealing, at best the picnic might have been fun, at worst it would have had none of the tension that charged the quiet air of the vlei. She had come to see the ducklings and she had seen them. Ordinarily she would have loved to stay here longer, now she wanted only to go back to Bronze Mountain. But that would be playing into Roan's hands, and the defiance that bubbled inside her made her rebel against that. Keeping her eyes on the water, she sat down on a rock, and wondered how far Roan's patience could be stretched.

The minutes passed. Fifteen minutes, perhaps twenty. Not a sound from behind her. If Roan felt irritation at the waiting game, he was not showing it.

The silence began, finally, to get on her nerves. She turned her head. He was lying on his back. His eyes were closed and his lashes made shadows on his cheeks. His hair had been rumpled by the wind, strands of it lay across his forehead. His lips, so often stern, always sensuous, were relaxed.

Megan was not surprised at the lump in her throat, at the way her heart reached out to him. It was one thing to acknowledge, intellectually, that between Roan and herself there could never be anything but animosity, or at best a formal kind of politeness. It was another to destroy the feelings that had rooted themselves so firmly the first day she had met him. She had tried, oh, she *had* tried to be unaffected by Roan, but without success.

I'll have to try harder, she told herself. He isn't for me. He can never be for me.

Watching him sleep was quite obviously not the way to destroy those feelings. From the first Megan had been impressed by Roan's maleness, by the aura of strength and power that were as much a part of him as his pipe and his rough-textured sweater. Later, when his attitude towards her had changed, she had become aware of an arrogance that she had not suspected, had tried to tell herself that it was a quality she despised. None of these qualities were apparent now. Stretched out on the ground, with the incongruous smudged shadows of his lashes softening the hard lines of his cheeks, Roan had the look of a man who could feel the pain and the sorrow and the inadequacies of lesser mortals than himself. He looked vulnerable, Megan decided wonderingly.

Since she had learned his identity, she had tried to think of him as Brendon Stevens—hard, unrepentant of the fact that his driving had resulted in a fatal accident, so indifferent to the grief of Tammy's family that a formal note had been his only contact with them. But the man she watched sleeping was not Brendon, he was Roan. Here at this vlei she had fallen in love with him. She loved him still, despite all reason, all logic, and she ached with the longing to touch him.

Was it only a week ago that they had been here together? Here in the clearing they had stood and watched the ducklings being hatched. And then Roan had kissed her, and she had responded to him with an ardour she had never dreamed she possessed. If only the clock could be turned back! Then they would still be Megan and Roan, two people without a past. And the magic would still envelop them.

Overcome by a feeling of sudden helplessness, she turned her head back to the water. She had to stop torturing herself, had to think of things other than Roan. There was no reason even to remain sitting here. He would be furious when he woke and found her gone, but he would not be surprised.

About to get to her feet, she heard him say, 'What are you thinking?'

She forced herself to keep her eyes on the water. 'I thought you were sleeping.'

A laugh sounded behind her, low and vital, and infinitely seductive. 'Ah!'

He hadn't been sleeping at all. Watching him, she had thought herself unobserved, and yet he had known all the time that she was watching him. She felt her cheeks grow warm.

'What were you thinking about, Megan?'

Something in his voice made her turn. He had lifted

himself on to one elbow, his body looked long and relaxed as it stretched out on the ground. His face had none of the hardness she had come to expect in him, and in his eyes was an expression that sent the blood racing through her veins.

It was hard to fight him when all she wanted was to lie down beside him and feel his arms close around her. Without pausing to think of the consequences, she said simply, 'I was remembering the first time we were here.'

Was it her imagination that the long body seemed to tighten? 'I see.'

'It was all so beautiful. The ducklings. And. . . .' She stopped.

'Our lovemaking,' he prompted softly.

The blood was pounding hard now. 'That too,' she acknowledged after a moment, bravely. And then, made daring by the intensity of his gaze, 'Have you ever wished that clocks could be turned back?'

What softness there had been in his face was gone as he jerked himself upright. 'Clocks can't be turned back.' His voice was so harsh that she flinched. 'Things happen, Megan, we can't change the things that happen.'

Don't go on, she wanted to say. I don't want to hear it.

'But people can change.' His tone had altered. 'Perceptions can change.' There was a strange light in the eyes that held hers. 'Do you believe that?'

I don't know what I believe. I know that you look haunted, tormented, and it pains me to see you like this.

'I don't know,' she said after a moment.

'We had something good starting for us, here at the vlei. Why does that have to change?'

Dimly she knew that there were answers she could give him, but her nerves were clamouring in response to the challenge he had thrown her. She could only look at him wordlessly.

He looked back at her for what seemed a long time, and she saw a muscle move convulsively in his throat. Then he had closed the gap between them and was holding her in his arms. She did not even try to get away from him as he kissed her—a tentative kiss, as if he was a little unsure of himself. After a moment he lifted his head and looked down at her, and his eyes still held the torment. He let out a groan, then he began to kiss her again. This time the kisses were deep and demanding, the sweetness so intense that she opened her mouth to him on a wild surge of pleasure.

I love you. The words clamoured in her heart and in her brain. Oh, Roan, I love you!

His kisses became more passionate, and she was returning them, kiss for kiss. She pressed herself against him as his hands began to move over her, sliding from her waist down to her hips, and then up over her breasts, shaping themselves to the soft curves of her body. She made no attempt to repulse him, she could *not* have done so, for in an echo of his evident desire she felt a longing of her own that was like nothing she had ever known.

With surprising gentleness he coaxed her on to the ground. She could feel the soft grass beneath her back, the roughness of pebbles beneath her legs. He knelt beside her, and when he had opened the buttons of her blouse he began to stroke her, her shoulders and her throat, and lastly her breasts, his hands curving around them, lingering on swelling nipples with a tenderness that was more erotic than the passion that had preceded it.

'You're so lovely,' he said raggedly, then he knelt back and began to unbutton his shirt.

Through a haze Megan watched him. She knew what was about to happen, and she was not frightened, though for her it would be the first time. How could she be frightened? She loved Roan, and there was a rightness about their lovemaking in this windswept secret place.

She was about to reach up her arms to him when he said, 'I'm glad you didn't go with Larry.' His eyes were filled with a mixture of tenderness and desire. Roan's eyes, looking at her from the face she saw every night in her dreams.

Brendon's eyes! The realisation hit her so suddenly that she flinched. The eyes of Brendon Stevens. While he had been kissing and caressing her he had been only Roan. Roan was the man to whom she had responded with such ardour. How in heaven could she have forgotten, even for a moment, that he was also Brendon Stevens, the one man she was forbidden to love?

'I'd have had a good time with Larry too.' Given the circumstances, it was the cruellest sentence she had ever uttered. It was also the most difficult.

She heard the raw hiss of breath. Roan had the look of a man who had been incredibly hurt. The look lasted only a second, then his mouth tightened and the lovely expression of tenderness was replaced by an icy contempt.

'You're even more like Tammy than I realised,' he said hardly.

'I asked you not to talk about her.'

'Why not? Do you think you set all the terms, Megan? Like you, your sister was a tease.'

What she would remember, with shame, was that at that moment she could only wonder what there had been between Tammy and Roan. Whether they had made love.

She blinked hard, as if by so doing she could erase an image that was too painful to contemplate. 'I'm not teasing,' she whispered.

'What do you call this little act?' His tone was like a whip, lashing into her with every syllable.

'You don't understand. . . .' She stopped. She could not tell him that she had wanted him to make love to her. That she had not been leading him on, for in those timeless moments he had been only Roan, a man with no past. That with every nerve and fibre of her being she longed to be in his arms again. Better for her if she could stop admitting the fact even to herself.

'So you think I don't understand,' he said through his teeth. 'I'm not stupid, Megan. All this has to do with Tammy's death. Did you think that by bringing out the animal in me and then pushing me from you, you were wreaking your own kind of revenge?'

'No.' She was trembling.

'Sex isn't a tool.' It was obvious that he did not believe her. 'Get dressed.'

Until the moment he said it she had not even been aware of her nakedness. 'When you've gone,' she said faintly.

'I thought we'd established that I'm not going without you.'

One look at his face was enough to know that he meant it. 'Turn your head,' she entreated.

'I'll look where I please.'

'Roan. . . .'

'And if you think that I'll touch you, don't bother to delude yourself!'

'Because you think I'm out for revenge,' the words came out painfully.

'Because, my dear'—a dismissive lift of an eyebrow—

'I've lost interest.' Mocking eyes raked her body. 'Get dressed Megan, and hurry up about it.'

Trembling hands slid the bra over her shoulders and fastened the clasp. Megan bent to retrieve her blouse, and as she straightened her eyes went involuntarily to Roan. He was not watching her after all. He was looking across the water. She could not see his face, but there was a tautness in his neck and shoulders. As she put on her blouse, glad of the respite which allowed her to dress unobserved, she wondered what he was thinking.

'Get much done?' asked Ann.

It was Tuesday, two days after the ill-fated morning at the vlei, and Megan was frustrated. She had spent hours in the recreation hall—hard work was an antidote to bruised feelings, wasn't it?—and there was disappointingly little to show for her efforts.

Putting down her coffee-mug, she gave a sigh. 'Almost nothing.'

'Something wrong?'

'Just a mild case of burn-out.'

'After not quite ten days? I don't believe it,' Ann said briskly. 'Like to talk about it?' And as Megan's head jerked up, 'You've been out of sorts since your outing on Sunday.'

Megan looked across the table in surprise. 'You noticed?'

'Fine friend I'd be if I hadn't.' Ann paused a moment, and when she went on her voice had gentled. 'Roan again?'

'How did you know?'

'Just a suspicion. I didn't know you'd gone out together, but someone saw you ride back with him.'

'We met at the vlei,' Megan confessed.

Ann looked astonished. 'I thought you were going alone. I drew you a map.'

'Right.'

'And you met by accident?'

Green eyes were thoughtful. 'Not by accident, not by arrangement either. The stableman told Roan I'd gone riding on my own and he . . . he was concerned.'

'How did he know where to find you?'

Megan picked up the mug and sipped her coffee without tasting it. 'I told you, we'd been there together that first day.'

'I remember.' Ann's eyes were compassionate. 'Something happened on Sunday, and it's clear it unsettled you.'

'It did.' Megan's voice shook.

'You've fallen in love with Roan?'

'No! At least. . . . Ann, it would be impossible, don't you see?'

'He's one heck of a man,' Ann said gently.

Megan stared at her. 'You can say that after what happened?'

'Of course.' Ann's tone was level. 'There was an accident. Roan was driving. Megan, my dear, we all grieved for Tammy, but accidents do happen, you know that.'

'Yes. . . .'

'You blame Roan.'

'He was driving,' Megan insisted.

'You don't know the details.'

Megan felt something quiver up her spine. 'Do you?'

Ann hesitated a moment, then said, 'No.'

Did Ann know something which Megan did not know? She was about to ask the question when Ann said, 'Why is it so impossible for you to let yourself like Roan? A terrible thing happened, granted, but he isn't a criminal.'

'I know.'

'Then why can't you forgive him? You've suffered, Megan, but Roan has suffered too.'

'Has he?' Megan said bitterly.

'You say that as if you don't believe me.'

'I believe Roan is a callous and unfeeling man,' Megan said carefully.

Ann looked at her incredulously. 'Roan—unfeeling? He's tough and strong, but he's also sensitive. I know he was devastated by the accident.'

'He had a fine way of showing it!'

'Perhaps,' Ann said quietly, 'you'd better tell me what you mean by that.'

'It's not easy.'

'I think it's necessary all the same. Why don't we top up the coffee first?'

Megan's chair faced the window, and while Ann poured fresh coffee, she looked outside. A mountain, not Bronze Mountain but another, rose behind the cabins of the resort. On its slopes, hidden in windswept willows, was the vlei, the place where she had experienced so many different emotions. She was seized by a sudden trembling which she tried to still, grateful that Ann was taking purposely long to come back to her. By the time her friend had seated herself, bare legs tucked casually beneath her on the chair, the trembling had ceased.

Slowly Megan began to speak. 'The shock of learning that Tammy had died. . . . I don't know if I can go into that. It's still too raw. . . .'

'Of course,' Ann agreed softly.

'We were notified by telephone. Someone called from the hospital—and from Bronze Mountain. All we could think of was Tammy, of the loss.'

She paused and put her hands over her eyes. The

scene was as vivid in her mind as if it had only just occurred. Dad, white and stunned, walking back from the phone with the terrible news. Mom, racked by grief. And Megan herself, numb, disbelieving at first, and then weeping until there were no tears left inside her.

Letting her hands fall back into her lap, she drew a shaky breath. 'It was only a day later that we began to wonder about the driver. All we knew was that he was all right. Every day we kept thinking that he would come to see us, but he never came.'

She paused again, and involuntarily her eyes went back to the slope. She could not see the vlei, did not even know its exact location, but she knew that it was there. Silly that she should have let herself get so carried away by her emotions. True, she had never been stirred by a man as she had been by Roan, had never felt quite so alive as when she was with him, so overwhelmingly feminine. But neither had she ever felt so torn between what her heart demanded and what her mind told her was right.

'One day a letter arrived.' Her voice was toneless now. 'More of a note, really—typed, expressing regret for the accident and our loss. Not even the signature at the end was written by hand.'

Ann's stifled exclamation escaped her as she went on. 'I can see it, Ann, even now. I just have to close my eyes and I can see that note. I know every word of it by memory, it was so short.'

'Megan. . . .'

'Formal—a duty note.' Megan passed a hand before her eyes. 'It might have been better if he hadn't bothered to write at all.' She looked across at her friend. 'Now perhaps you can understand when I say that Roan is callous and unfeeling.'

'I understand why you think it.'

Megan's head jerked up as Ann put down her mug and got to her feet. She watched her friend go to the window. When she turned back there was a thoughtful look in her face, intense sympathy in her eyes.

'Time that you heard the other side of the story, Megan.'

'The . . . other side?' queried Megan.

'Not all of it, because I don't know it all. You asked me if I knew the details of the accident—I don't know them all. I do know that Roan was a good driver, fast sometimes perhaps, but never reckless.'

'What are you trying to say?' Megan whispered through white lips.

'This isn't easy for me, but I have to say it. Tammy led Roan a merry dance.'

'No!'

'I'm afraid so. And Roan isn't a man to be made a fool of.'

'You're saying something happened between them the night of the accident?'

'I think so.' Ann hesitated. 'I've heard that. . . .' She stopped. 'It's no use going on about it. I don't know what happened, and Roan has never been willing to talk.'

'But you wanted me to know all the same.'

'Only because you shouldn't judge him without knowing the facts.' Ann paused, and when she went on the look of sympathy had deepened. 'As for the note, don't judge him on that score either.'

'There *is* something I don't know.'

'Yes, there is. Megan, Roan was not all right. He was alive, yes, but he was hurt—quite badly hurt.'

'I didn't know! Nobody told us.'

'He was in hospital. For three months he was virtually immobile.'

'We didn't know,' Megan said brokenly.

'He couldn't have gone to see you. He couldn't even have written to you. One of the nurses must have typed the letter for him.'

'We didn't know,' Megan said again. 'Why weren't we told?'

'Thoughtlessness, I suppose. And the fact that you already had so much to grieve you.'

'There was communication with Bronze Mountain. Someone from the office.' Megan was shaking. 'There was no lack of sympathy. But nobody told us about Roan.'

'It's appalling!' Ann looked distressed. 'We should have thought to tell you—but somehow we didn't. We thought we were doing the right thing.'

'Poor Roan,' Megan said at last.

'Yes, my dear, poor Roan.'

Caught by Ann's voice, Megan looked up. 'There's more, isn't there?'

'I'm afraid so.' Ann looked grim. 'Not only Roan's body was injured, but he became very depressed. For a long while he seemed to withdraw into himself.'

'He's not withdrawn now.'

'He's been much better since he left the hospital, the outdoor life seems to be good for him. But, Megan, he's lost his confidence in himself.'

Megan stared. 'He doesn't give that impression.'

'Roan was always a strong man—outwardly nothing much has changed.'

'Then how can you be so sure?'

'For one thing,' said Ann, 'he avoids driving a car.'

'He's usually on horseback,' Megan acknowledged after a moment.

'Now you know why.'

'Does he never drive?'

'At the beginning, when he came out of the hospital, he didn't. He does now. But not often, and then only when he's alone.'

Memory struck. 'He offered to drive me.'

'He did?' The other girl's voice was alive with interest.

'That first evening, after we'd got to Bronze Mountain. He offered to drive me to the station to pick up my luggage.' Megan paused. 'You look surprised.'

'I am. To my knowledge he's driven nobody since the accident.'

'Are you sure?'

'As sure as I can be.' Quietly Ann said, 'You must have made an impression on him.'

'We had something good going for us,' Roan had said, referring to the day they had spent together, when each had been in blissful ignorance of the other's identity. Oh, it *had* been good! So very good.

'We'd spent the day together,' Megan said, painfully. 'But you know that.'

'You didn't know who Roan was then.'

'Nor did he know that I was Tammy's sister.'

'What a mess!' Ann burst out with sudden vehemence, almost as if she was aware of what had actually happened. 'And you refused Roan's offer to drive you, I suppose.'

'Larry had offered by then,' Megan said awkwardly.

'And you'd discovered that Roan was Brendon Stevens.'

'. . . Yes. I regret it now, but at the time—I wonder if you can understand—I couldn't bring myself to go with him.'

'I do understand,' Ann said very gently. 'I also understand that, without meaning to, you may have driven the last nail into the coffin of Roan's confidence.'

CHAPTER FIVE

LONG after the cabin was silent Megan lay sleepless. Restlessly she tossed beneath the sheets. Roan's face was before her eyes, and when she closed them he was in her mind. The strong-boned face, not handsome in a conventional sense, and yet more attractive than any she had ever known. The laughter lines around the eyes, the well-defined brows, the uncompromising chin— every feature of Roan's face was imprinted on her mind as clearly as if she was studying a photograph.

The look of torment, she saw that too. And she was swept with pain at the thought of his suffering. That Roan, the most compelling man she had ever met, should have lost his confidence was hard to believe. Yet after the talk with Ann, believe it Megan did.

Restlessly Megan tossed between the sheets. After a while, knowing that she would not sleep, she got out of bed, slipped into thick sweater and jeans, and quietly left the cabin. It was very dark outside. In sharp contrast to the heat of the day it was also cold, so that Megan was glad of her warm sweater.

When her eyes had accustomed themselves to the dark, she began to walk along the path that led away from the cabin and towards the canyon. The night was sweet with the scent of tropical shrubs and wild flowers, and the air rang with the sound of crickets. It was so lovely out of doors that she felt some of the restlessness draining from her.

Knowing how easy it would be to slip on the rocky path, she did not walk far, certainly not as far as the edge of the cliffs. Coming to a viewpoint she recognised, she stopped and looked about her. The sky was a blaze of stars, and the moon was a slender crescent. Against the sky were the mountains, a bulky mass of intense blackness, brooding and remote.

The cool grandeur of the scene was balm to raw nerves. In the cabin she had been unable to think, but her mind seemed clearer now.

She had driven the last nail into the coffin of Roan's confidence, Ann had said. Perhaps she really had done just that. Such being the case, it was up to her to make amends. If she was certain of nothing else, she knew that.

Once before she had written a mental letter to her parents, one she had never put on paper, never posted. In the cool dark night she began to compose another letter. 'Tammy can never be brought back to life,' she began. 'It's a fact we have to accept, and learn to live with. But there's something else I have to live with, something that affects only me. I love Roan. I loved him before I knew that he was Brendon Stevens, and I love him still. You have to understand that, Mom and Dad. We thought of him as some kind of monster, but he was never that. He didn't visit us because he was in no state to, and the note was typewritten because someone had to do it for him. Even the words may have stemmed from one of the nurses. We don't know what happened the night of the accident. We may never know, but Ann—as fine a person as you could wish to meet—has only respect for Roan. You'll never meet the man I love, because I know I have no future with him. But one thing I do know: my beloved Roan has lost his confidence, and I'm going to help him get it back.'

Like the other letter it was one she would never post. It did not matter. Composing the words in her mind had given her a sense of perspective and direction. She now knew what she must do.

Next morning she attacked the recreation-hall wall with enthusiasm. The lethargy and indecision of the last two days was gone. Creativity surged inside her, and she worked with zest. The wall would look wonderful when it was finished. Tammy's creation, executed by her sister, but Tammy's creation notwithstanding. A mural that was in keeping with Bronze Mountain, in as much as trees and space and vastness all had their place. A mural that was bold and modern in concept, and which blended with the lovely liquid lines of the hall.

By coming to Bronze Mountain, Megan had ensured that Tammy's memory would live. There was no cause to feel disloyal because it was now time to think of Roan too.

He was working at the site where the dam would be, she found out. Noon should be a good time to see him, for the men would be breaking for lunch.

The stableman looked dubious when she asked him for a horse. 'I'm not going far,' she smiled at him, knowing that he was thinking of the day when she had ridden to the vlei.

'In the veld?'

'Just down to the site.'

When the resort was finished there would be a dam near the foot of Bronze Mountain. It would be stocked with fish, and there would be boating and fishing for most of the year. In the evening, when the setting sun gilded Bronze Mountain, it would send its glow over the water. Though the dam was some distance from the cabins, Megan sensed that it would become a focal point for visitors to the resort.

Arriving at the dam she found the men still at work;

evidently she had not timed the lunch-break as accurately as she had imagined. At the excavation site a group of labourers swung their picks, arms lifting and falling in unison to the rhythm of the song that they chanted. A littler farther away a group of engineers stood with their measuring instruments.

Megan saw Roan immediately. He was talking to the engineers, and judging by the attentive way they were listening it was evident that he had their respect. He was a man who would always command respect, Megan thought, watching him; respect in other men, and respect mingled with an almost inevitable sexual excitement in women, for surely the woman did not exist who would be completely immune to his appeal. Tall and strong and powerful, he reminded her of a jungle animal. His head was tilted to one side in a manner she recognised, and suddenly he laughed, the sound vital and amused. A lump came suddenly to Megan's throat. Seeing him like this, it hurt her to know that inside him there was a core of suffering.

'Roan!' she called when he moved away from the group.

At the sound of his name he looked up. And then he grinned and waved a hand. 'Why, Megan! I'll be right up.'

It was absurd that it took no more than a grin to make her feel happy. For the first time she allowed herself to acknowledge that she had been uncertain of her reception. After what had happened between them at the vlei she had not known what to expect.

'This is a surprise,' he observed as he reached her.

She needed no help dismounting, but he was helping her anyway, and as she felt his hands on her waist a familiar quiver shot through her. 'A nice one, I hope.' She tried to keep the tremor from her voice.

'Very.' The hands that held her waist tightened a fraction, but his voice was teasingly light. 'It's always nice to be visited by a beautiful woman.'

How many other women had visited him when he was working? She pushed away the thought. Silly that she could not bear the idea of Roan with other women.

'And what brings you here, Megan?'

She looked up at him. He was still holding her, apparently oblivious of what anyone who was watching them might infer. He was so close to her that she could see the tiny dark specks in the brown of his eyes. He wore a safari suit, sleeves rolled up to the elbows, and she could see the muscles of tanned arms, and in the vee of his jacket, beneath his throat, the hairs that curled at the top of his chest. The longing to be held against that chest was unexpectedly fierce, and her breathing was suddenly shallow.

'I wanted to talk to you.'

The hands on her waist grew a little rigid, the brown eyes took on a speculative expression. 'Sure.' Letting go of her, he gestured to a clump of acacias. 'You'll find it cooler in the shade over there.'

She was acutely aware of him as he walked at her side. Once his arm brushed hers, and she felt her skin burn where he had touched it. Again the longing welled in her, the desire to be in his arms, to make love with him. 'I feel as I've never really lived before,' she wrote in the mental letter to her parents, 'I've never known what it was to feel quite so feminine.'

'What's on your mind?' asked Roan when they reached the trees.

'The accident.'

His tone changed as he took a step away from her. 'We've said all there is to say about that.'

'No, Roan, wait!' She put an urgent hand on his arm,

and felt him grow tense. 'You were in hospital.'

After a moment he said aloofly, 'So?'

'You were in hospital a few months. You couldn't have visited us. You couldn't even write.'

'Someone's been telling tales,' he said drily.

'You had to dictate the note to us.'

'Ann?'

'Why didn't you tell us, Roan?'

He touched her throat, she could feel the long fingers at the base of it. 'Should I have told you?'

Under his fingers her pulse beat a crazy tattoo. 'Of course you should have! We would have understood.'

'Why I didn't show more concern, is that what you mean?'

'I suppose so,' she agreed, a little more uncertainly.

The hand moved, going upwards, sliding beneath her hair. 'You'd have hated me less?'

How easy it would be now to say they had never hated him. But it wouldn't be true, and Roan would know it. 'We'd have understood your silence.'

'Perhaps.'

'At least. . . . When we met, why didn't you tell me then?'

'When we met,' he said very softly, and his fingers played in her hair with a sensuousness that was almost unbearable, 'I didn't know that Megan was Tammy's sister.'

'Later you did.'

'Later. Ah.' The fingers tightened. 'By then you didn't want to hear.'

'That's not true.'

'Isn't it?' He was stroking her face now, the movement slow and tantalising. 'If you remember, I invited you to dinner, and you declined.'

Appalled, she did remember. 'You would have told me then?'

'Probably.' A finger traced the contours of her lips. Then he said, 'Fool that I'd have been.'

Caught by the tone as much as the words, Megan jerked back to look at him. The expression in his eyes took her breath away. He looked so hard, so cynical. Could a man be both cynical and sensuous at the same time?

'I don't understand,' she said jerkily.

'It's not difficult. You'd cast me in the part of the villain. Nothing I could have told you would have made any difference.'

Was that true? Megan recalled her outrage on discovering that Roan was Brendon Stevens. 'It makes a difference now.' Her tone was low.

He cupped her chin, tilting her head. She was so close to him that she sensed every inch of the sinuous body, though she was not in contact with it. She held her breath, wondering if he meant to kiss her.

Instead he said, 'Poor Megan.'

'Poor Megan? What do you mean?' And then, when he didn't answer, 'Is it too late?'

'Too late for what?'

Damn you, Roan, do you have to make me spell it out? Do you take pleasure in punishing me? 'For us to be. . . .' She hesitated over the last word, then got out 'friends'.

Roan gave a mirthless laugh, and she knew the hesitation hadn't escaped him.

'I just wanted to tell you that I'm sorry,' she said huskily, and saw his lips curl. 'Sorry that I misjudged you. That we all three misjudged you, my parents and I. Can't you accept that?'

'I suppose it would be churlish of me to do anything else.'

She took a step towards him. 'Roan. . . .'

He ignored her pleading. 'Why did you come to see me here? What was so important that it couldn't wait?'

Hadn't she made it clear? Everything had seemed so easy, in the darkness, when she had stood looking towards the canyon and had made her decision.

'I wanted to apologise. To tell you that I know that accidents happen and that I have confidence in you.'

There was no softening in his face. 'That's a touching speech, Megan.'

'Did I come down here for nothing?' She felt a little ill.

'That depends on your expectations. Did you think you'd say your piece and we would then fall into each other's arms and be—what was the word?—friends?'

It was the gist of what she had planned. 'Something like that.'

He gripped her shoulders, bringing her close against him. 'You're like a little girl, Megan. You're twenty-three and you still believe in fairy-tales. And-they-all-lived-happily-ever-after endings. Life isn't like that.'

'It could be,' she flung at him recklessly.

'No.' His fingers bit into her flesh, hurting her. 'For you everything is suddenly clear. You've decided to forgive the fact that I didn't write you a personal note, that I didn't visit your family. You want to be—friends. Does it occur to you that I might have my own doubts, my own anger?'

She had been so sure that he would be relieved at her forgiveness. Had imagined him kissing her, talking of a new start to their relationship. This was nothing like the scene she had imagined.

She shook her head. 'You said we had something good going for us.'

'You're a very pretty girl, Megan.'

'You say that as if I was just a diversion.'

He shrugged. 'You said it, I didn't.'

Anger whipped her then. Lifting her hand, she struck him hard across one cheek. He took a step back in surprise, and in that moment she twisted away from him.

'Megan!' he shouted after her as she ran down the slope in the direction of the horse.

She heard him, but didn't stop. Rage was a tangible thing inside her, driving her on, even though her eyes were so blurred with tears that she could hardly see. All she wanted was to leave the dam-site, to get away from Roan, away from a humiliation that she had never envisaged.

'Megan!'

She ran faster. She didn't see the stone in her path. Her foot landed on it, and she slid sideways. As she hit the ground, she let out a cry of pain.

'Megan!' Roan was beside her in seconds. 'Are you all right, little one?'

Through the pain she heard the tenderness. 'I'm not sure.' She tried to get up, and gasped with pain. 'My foot!'

In an instant his arm was around her, and he was gentling her back on to the ground. 'Careful,' he told her, still in that same tender voice. 'Lean back against me, take some of the weight off your foot.'

She tried to push away. 'I don't want to.'

'I won't hurt you—don't you know that?'

She did know it. But something drove her to say, 'No. Where was your gentleness when we were talking?'

'That was different, and you know that too.' His voice was rough.

She knew too that despite all that had passed between them it was bliss to lie against his chest, to feel the beating of his heart, and the hardness of his muscles against her back.

She tried to push herself away from him. 'I have to go.'

'Not until I've taken a look at that foot. Don't be silly, Megan'—his voice was impatient as an arm tightened around her—'keep still, even if it bothers you to be close to me a few seconds.'

I would like to be close to you always. There are things *you* don't know either, Roan.

There was no option but to remain still as he eased her carefully back on to the ground so that he could bend to see her foot. The fingers that ran over her ankle were gentle. You're warm and kind and caring, Megan sent the words to him silently, wishing she could say them aloud, aware that now was not the time.

'You've sprained your ankle.' He lifted his head to look at her, and she saw that his eyes were bleak. 'You can't go back the way you came, you couldn't put that foot in a stirrup. There's a jeep at the site.'

'You'll drive me, Roan?'

'I'll get one of the men.'

'I want *you* to drive me.'

'I'm still busy with something.' He stood up. 'I'll give one of the men a shout. Anton will take you back to Bronze Mountain, he's one of the engineers.'

About to argue, Megan looked up at Roan's face, and the expression she saw there made her catch her breath. It was as if a mask had settled over the hard-boned features, making him as impersonal as a stranger. She felt suddenly cold.

She did not attempt to resist as he scooped her into his arms and began to carry her down the slope. For the moment the will to resist him had left her.

Anton was a lanky young man with a mop of red hair and a friendly face. 'I'll take care of her,' he said when Roan had put Megan down on the seat of the jeep.

She made one last attempt. 'Roan. . . .'

But Roan's expression was as impassive as if he had not heard her. 'Let Ann have a look at that foot,' was all he said.

'You're a good nurse,' Megan said gratefully.

Ann smiled as she put the last touches to the compress. 'Your foot will be fine in a day or two.'

'I wish I could say as much for my peace of mind,' sighed Megan. 'My plan misfired.'

'Want to tell me about it?'

'It might help.'

'Tell you what,' Ann stood up, 'I hear the kettle boiling. I'll make some coffee, that's always a good panacea, and then we'll talk.'

When Ann had left the bedroom, Megan leaned back her head on the pillow and closed her eyes. Her foot was throbbing and she felt tired. But she knew she would not sleep until she had made some sense of her muddled thoughts.

It was not hard to bring Roan into her mind. He intruded there at the strangest times, with no difficulty at all, she acknowledged wryly. Too often, in fact, if she was to have any measure of happiness when she left Bronze Mountain.

The Roan she saw now was the man at the dam-site, tall and aloof, sensuous and arrogant. Not the man she had thought of last night, a vulnerable man who had been robbed of his confidence. The Roan who had thrown her apologies back at her, who had accused her of believing in fairy-tales, was hard and self-sufficient. Tormented he might be, but if there was a quality that he lacked it did not seem to be confidence. Except in one area, supposing **Ann** was right about that.

Ann came back into the room with two steaming mugs of coffee and a plate of biscuits, and Megan began to talk.

'The whole thing was a mess,' she confided at last. 'I thought it would be so easy.'

'Nothing is ever quite so easy.'

'Almost what Roan said. He didn't want my apologies.'

'Perhaps he's not ready for them.'

'I told him I had confidence in his driving, and yet he asked Anton to drive me back to the cabin.' Megan looked thoughtful. 'I've thought about that. Roan said he was busy. Do you think that was the reason?'

'I know it wasn't. Roan is not accountable to anyone.'

'Because he's the chief engineer at Bronze Mountain?'

For the first time Ann seemed to hesitate. 'He's more than that Megan. Roan owns Bronze Mountain.'

'I didn't know that!'

'Not many people do.'

Megan looked at her friend curiously. 'He confides in you?'

'Sometimes. Roan and I go back some way together. I've done the landscaping for some of his other projects.'

'Bronze Mountain isn't his only resort, then?'

'There are at least three others.' Again Ann seemed to hesitate. 'Perhaps I shouldn't have told you, but I thought in the circumstances you should know a little more about Roan.'

'I'm glad you told me.' Megan tried to ignore the hollow sensation in the pit of her stomach. If circumstances had put Roan beyond her reach, his money and status now seemed to make him totally inaccessible. 'I'm surprised nobody else mentioned the fact—Larry, Anton.'

'They might not know—probably don't. Roan is an engineer by profession. He likes to work himself on each current project, and that's easier done if he can be on an equal footing with his men.'

There was a little silence after Ann's words. The girl seemed to understand that Megan had the need to digest what she had learned.

At last Megan said, 'Nobody would have minded if Roan had gone off.'

'That's right.'

'He didn't want to drive me.'

'Perhaps,' her friend said steadily, 'he wasn't able to.'

Megan's head lifted quickly. 'I told him I'd misjudged him, that I had confidence in him.'

'Could be he needs more than words.'

'What, Ann—what?'

'I'm not sure.'

'Roan is a strong man. He'll work through this problem on his own.'

'You may be right.'

Ann's noncommittal tone did not escape Megan. 'You think I should help him.'

'I think,' said Ann, 'you may be the only person who can do so.'

'I tried.' Megan pushed a hand through her hair. 'I apologised. I told him I had confidence in him. But he was so angry, so cynical.'

'Perhaps words are not enough.'

'What else can I do?'

'I don't know.' Ann got to her feet and picked up the coffee mugs. 'You won't solve it right now. You look dead beat, why don't you get some sleep before you try to do anything at all?'

It was the sound of the door opening that woke her. The head on the pillow felt heavy. It was all Megan could do to open her eyes a mere slit.

Roan had come into the room. She could just see his face, and on it was an expression that made her wonder if she was in fact asleep after all, if this was just a dream. Confused, she lay still. She thought she should sit up, should say something, but she felt drugged with sleep and with the pain-killer Ann had given her, and she could do nothing at all.

After a few moments Roan came slowly to her bed. Without lifting her head and opening her eyes fully, she could no longer see his face. Through the half-closed slits she could make out only his thighs and his waist. The confusion had cleared a little now, so that she might have been able to open her eyes all the way had she chosen to. But something stopped her.

The mist had cleared from her mind, and she remembered only too well all that had happened today. With certainty she knew that Roan thought her asleep, that he would not be at her bed if he had the faintest suspicion that she was awake. What was he up to she did not know, nor how long he would stay. But there was a magic intimacy in these moments which she wanted to preserve.

Lying quite still, she kept her breathing low and even—no easy feat when her senses had set up a wild clamouring. Even more difficult when a hand touched her cheek, a hand that was feather-light. It brushed once across her cheek, caressingly, then gently pushed a strand of hair from her forehead. Megan's heart was beating so wildly now that it was a struggle to keep her breathing steady and regular, but somehow she did so. Roan had allowed himself this tenderness only because he thought himself unobserved; not for anything would she disillusion him now.

He murmured something just under his breath, and except for her name, Megan, she did not catch the words. Then the hand was gone from her face and he was walking to the door. Moments later she heard the outer door of the cabin shut.

Long after he had gone she continued to lie still. Happiness filled her, welled inside her so that she felt as if her chest would burst. Roan might not reciprocate the love she felt for him, but he did not hate her as she had thought he did after what had happened today. The caress on her cheek, the tender brushing aside of her hair, these were not the actions of a man who hated.

He was an enigma. While she understood the nature of his torment she could not fathom the depths of it. Perhaps she had been naïve to think that just a few words from her would be enough to give him back his confidence, but in time she would be successful. She knew that quite certainly now.

A little later there was a knock at the door, and she called out happily, 'Come in,' thinking it would be either Roan again, or Ann. It was Larry, and he carried a bouquet of wild flowers.

'Best I could do,' he smiled down at her. 'How's the foot?'

'Fine. How did you know about it?'

'News travels fast, if you don't mind the cliché. Heard that you'd had an argument with Roan.'

'News also gets distorted. The part about Roan isn't true.' She spoke lightly, but she wondered how much people knew of what had occurred; how much the men at the site had overheard. Not the words themselves, it

Say Hello to Yesterday
Holly Weston had done it all alone.

She had raised her small son and worked her way up to features writer for a major newspaper. Still the bitterness of the of the past seven years lingered.

She had been very young when she married Nick Falconer—but old enough to lose her heart completely when he left. Despite her success in her new life, her old one haunted her.

But it was over and done with—until an assignment in Greece brought her face to face with Nick, and all she was trying to forget. . . .

Time of the Temptress
The game must be played his way!

Rebellion against a cushioned, controlled life had landed Eve Tarrant in Africa. Now only the tough mercenary Wade O'Mara stood between her and possible death in the wild, revolution-torn jungle.

But the real danger was Wade himself—he had made Eve aware of herself as a woman.

"I saved your neck, so you feel you owe me something," Wade said. "But you don't owe me a thing, Eve. Get away from me." She knew she could make him lose his head if she tried. But that wouldn't solve anything. . . .

Your Romantic Adventure Starts Here.

Born Out of Love
It had to be coincidence!

Charlotte stared at the man through a mist of confusion. It was Logan. An older Logan, of course, but unmistakably the man who had ravaged her emotions and then abandoned her all those years ago.

She ought to feel angry. She ought to feel resentful and cheated. Instead, she was apprehensive—terrified at the complications he could create.

"We are not through, Charlotte," he told her flatly. "I sometimes think we haven't even begun."

Man's World
Kate was finished with love for good.

Kate's new boss, features editor Eliot Holman, might have devastating charms—but Kate couldn't care less, even if it was obvious that he was interested in her.

Everyone, including Eliot, thought Kate was grieving over the loss of her husband, Toby. She kept it a carefully guarded secret just how cruelly Toby had treated her and how terrified she was of trusting men again.

But Eliot refused to leave her alone, which only served to infuriate her. He was no different from any other man. . . or was he?

These FOUR free Harlequin Presents novels allow you to enter the world of romance, love and desire. As a member of the Harlequin Home Subscription Plan, you can continue to experience all the moods of love. You'll be inspired by moments so real...so moving...you won't want them to end. So start your own Harlequin Presents adventure by returning the reply card below. <u>DO IT TODAY!</u>

BUSINESS REPLY CARD

First Class   Permit No. 70   Tempe, AZ

POSTAGE WILL BE PAID BY ADDRESSEE

Harlequin Reader Service
2504 W. Southern Avenue,
Tempe, Arizona 85282

NO POSTAGE
NECESSARY
IF MAILED
IN THE
UNITED STATES

would have been impossible for them to hear those, but the angry lift of her voice perhaps, and—Heaven forbid! and her cheeks warmed at the thought—the stinging sound of her slap.

Fortunately Larry was not one to dwell on matters that others were loath to discuss. He was also resourceful and entertaining. When he had made her some coffee—one cabin kitchen was much like another and he could find his way around in the dark, he said—he came to sit by her bed and regaled her with funny stories.

'I don't believe a word,' she laughed after one of his more outrageous anecdotes.

His lips pulled down in mock offence. 'I'm very hurt, my lady.'

'No, you're not. Larry, you're incorrigible!'

'Tammy thought so too.'

'Tammy?' She looked at him in surprise, the laughter fading. 'You say that as if you were friendly with my sister?'

Something shifted in his eyes. 'I knew your sister, naturally, it's not the first time I've mentioned her.'

'Just the way you spoke. . . .'

'I'm friendly with everyone at Bronze Mountain. Almost.' He grinned, the infectious grin that was one of his most appealing features. 'Here's one you haven't heard, Megan. There was this girl, and she thought it would be a good idea to go swimming in a rock pool on Bronze Mountain. Trouble was, she didn't have a bathing-suit. . . .'

It was a naughty story, and one Megan knew he had made up, but it was also very funny and not at all in bad taste.

'That was lovely,' she said, wiping the laughter tears from her eyes. 'You're a tremendous sickbed visitor.'

'And you,' he said, bending towards her and

dropping a kiss full on her lips, 'are the sweetest sickbed person to visit.'

A little startled, she was also amused by the kiss, which had meant nothing to either of them. 'You're taking advantage of a poor immobile girl.'

'A very beautiful immobile girl.' Surprisingly there was no echoing laughter in his eyes. 'And I may just take advantage of her helpless state to claim another kiss.'

Megan thought afterwards it was the muttered exclamation which had her swinging round just as Larry was bending towards her. 'Roan!' she called gladly, at sight of the tall figure who had come unnoticed into the room.

'Megan. Larry.' A formal acknowledgment.

'Won't you sit down?' She gestured towards the other chair by her bed. And when he made no move, 'The coffee's still hot, isn't it, Larry?'

'Sure is.' Larry glanced at Roan.

'Don't bother.' Roan's lips were set, and the long jaw had a hard line to it.

'No bother,' said Larry, and Megan wondered at the unholy gleam in the younger man's eyes. 'I don't mind bringing you a mug. I'm quite at home here.'

'So I see,' Roan observed harshly, as he made for the door.

'Won't you stay?' Megan asked, unaware of the pleading in her tone, knowing only that the happiness which had been with her since his earlier appearance in the room was fast fading.

'No.'

'Roan. . . .'

'I came to find out how you are, and I see that you're fine.'

'Sure about the coffee?' Larry put in, and Megan

had the uncomfortable feeling that he was goading Roan.

'Of course.'

Megan watched him go, tall and overwhelmingly male, attractive even when he was angry. For he was angry now. A very different man from the tender Roan who had stood by her bed when he'd thought her asleep. It was not hard to guess at the cause of his anger. She did not know how long he had been in the room, how much of the conversation he had overheard, but he had taken in the last part, had certainly seen the kiss.

'You misconstrued what you saw,' she had wanted to tell him. 'Larry was joking, I mean nothing to him. As for his kiss, I didn't feel it. It didn't affect me one way or another.' But she had kept silent. There were certain situations when thoughts could not be put into words.

'Have you heard the one about the man and the bananas?' she heard Larry ask. Until now she had been amused by his jokes, all at once she could not bear to hear even one more.

'Another time.' She tried to smile. 'I'm a little tired.'

'Roan has that much effect on you?' She had not known that Larry could sound sulky.

'Don't be silly. I'm tired, it's been quite a day.'

'Don't go falling for him, Megan. There's no happiness in it. Tammy found that out to her cost.'

She flinched, and put out a hand. 'Please, Larry, don't!'

'Sorry, that was tasteless of me, I suppose.' He gave a short laugh. 'I didn't mean just the accident. Roan isn't the kind of man to have only one girl in his life. He's still seeing Petra for one.'

Megan remembered the girl who had been with him in the restaurant on that first night. She had seen her talking to Roan, walking with him sometimes, since then. She wondered if Larry knew that he was rubbing salt in a wound that was already too raw.

'I'm a little tired,' she said again, more firmly this time. 'It was kind of you to come, Larry, but now I'd really like to be alone.'

CHAPTER SIX

THERE were days when Megan wondered whether she had in fact dreamed the little episode by her bed. The tenderness she had sensed in Roan then was something she never saw again. He never came again to her cabin; it was as if the scene he had witnessed with Larry had convinced him that there was nothing much wrong with her.

And indeed, one more day spent in bed was all the rest her foot needed. After that she was able to walk once more, though with some care, as the ankle was still sensitive if she put weight on it quickly.

It was good to be back at work. With Ann out most of the day it was lonely in the cabin. Besides, work was a kind of therapy. Sometimes, when she sloshed paint on the wall with unnecessary vigour, Megan knew that she was unleashing her feelings of frustration.

Frustrated she certainly was. A few weeks more and she would be leaving Bronze Mountain. Roan had to be at ease in a car before then. There was a time when she had thought her objective so simple. Now she had begun to wonder whether she would ever achieve it.

She saw Roan now and then; it would be impossible not to see a person in a place the size of Bronze Mountain. Mostly he did not stop, his only acknowledgment a brief, 'Hello, Megan,' spoken in mid-step.

'I'm going to pin him down if it kills me,' she told Ann once, grimly. 'He is *the* most infuriating man I've ever met!'

'He's made quite an impact on you.'

'He's arrogant and self-sufficient.'

'And sexy,' Ann put in with a smile.

'Sexy too,' Megan acknowledged after a moment. 'He also has more confidence than any man I ever met.'

'Except when it comes to driving.'

There it was again. Ann liked Roan, she had empathy with him, and she seemed to feel that Megan was the only one who could help him. If only Megan herself was not beginning to feel more and more dubious about her chances.

At a staff barbecue she decided to take the matter in hand. Roan was standing alone when she approached him. After a few moments of small-talk she went straight to the point. 'Been to the vlei lately, Roan?'

Something flickered in his eyes. 'No.'

'Have you wondered about the ducklings?'

His gaze was cool. 'I've had other things on my mind. Care for a drink, Megan?'

He would leave her, ostensibly to get her a drink, in fact to change the subject and get away from her, for on his way he would see to it that he was sidetracked. A good ploy, but one that she would not fall for.

'No drink just yet, thank you. Do you know, I'd love to visit the vlei again, see how the ducklings have grown.'

'You were thinking of riding that way?' He frowned imperiously. 'I don't want you riding alone in the veld, you know that.'

Ann doesn't consider you are arrogant. I wonder if she knows you at all.

'My foot isn't up to being in a stirrup yet.' Not true, she would manage to ride very well. 'There's a road that goes that way, isn't there? I was thinking it would be really nice to take a drive out that way.

'On your own?' One eyebrow had lifted.

Her heart was beating too fast. They were playing games, she and Roan, and they were games that did not come naturally to her. His eyes lingered on her face a moment before moving downwards, and she wondered if he could see the pulse beating at the base of her throat.

'I don't have a car. Would you drive me?' She smiled up at him. It was a smile that had made an impact on more than one male in the past, but Roan looked unimpressed.

'Afraid not.' His tone was without inflection.

'I'd really love to go to the vlei.'

The eyes that met hers were hard. 'Have you asked Larry to take you there? I've no doubt he would be happy to oblige.'

'Maybe so,' she said softly, 'but do you really want me to go with Larry to the vlei?'

'You know how to pack your punches, don't you?' He spoke with quiet contempt. 'If we went to the vlei together, Megan, my mind wouldn't be on the ducklings.'

It was useless pretending she did not understand his meaning. 'You don't make things easy,' she said, over the thudding in her ears.

'You started this.' Roan grinned, but without humour. 'Sure you don't want that drink?—because I do. Remember to say hello to the ducks for me when you go, will you?'

She watched him walk away, and her fingers curled into her palms in a mixture of anger and frustration. How much could she take of this? And did she really have to go on with it?

Leaving the recreation hall one evening, she saw the Bronze Mountain car drive by. Roan was at the wheel, and he was alone. So he had no problem with driving in itself, she thought, as she watched the car go round a corner. It was the idea of passengers which gave him trouble.

It was time for her to try again.

Bronze Mountain was like a village in the sense that snippets of news became quickly known. Several people had access to the resort car. It was not hard to find out when Roan intended using it, or that he was driving to a near-by town to do some research.

'I'd like a lift into town with you,' she told him matter-of-factly, with none of the coyness she had used the last time, and which she did not enjoy.

'No, Megan.'

'I need some supplies.'

'You heard me.'

It was time to be direct. 'I think you should take me.'

'What are you trying to prove?' he asked through his teeth. He was holding a pencil, and his fingers curled around it with such force that she thought it might break. 'Trying to show me how brave you are?'

She kept her voice light. 'I want supplies, and you happen to be driving to town.'

His mouth twisted. 'And you just happen to choose for a driver the man who killed your sister.'

'Don't say that!'

'Why not? It's on both our minds.' Without warning he caught her arms in his hands, filling her with excitement despite the fact that the gesture was anything but lover-like. The line of his mouth was inflexible. 'I don't know what you're playing at,' he said harshly. 'Just leave me alone, Megan, it's all I ask.'

They stood staring at each other. Megan's breathing was shallow, Roan's was ragged. They stood motionless a full minute, neither of them saying a word. Then Megan tried to twist away, but Roan's grip was unrelenting. She tried to shift her eyes from his, and found she could not. She could hear her heart beating, and wondered if he could hear it too.

The dark head came down suddenly. Roan's lips were hard, bruising. The kiss, if it could be called a kiss, lasted only a few seconds. Then he had jerked away, as if her lips burned, and he released her arms, pushing her from him.

'Leave me alone,' he ground out, before wheeling away.

Leave him alone—she wanted to do just that. As she wandered alone in the dark after supper, Megan kept reliving the moments when Roan's lips had punished hers—for that was what it had been, sheer punishment for them both. After what had happened she wanted nothing more than to leave Bronze Mountain. It would be agony to stay here day after day, and to know that every time she saw Roan he looked at her with hatred.

Yet she could not leave Bronze Mountain until the mural was finished. Nor could she leave Roan alone—it would be the coward's way out if she did. He would hate her now whatever happened, she was convinced of that. But she loved him. And loving him, she would not leave him until she had given him the one thing that he could perhaps get from nobody else.

The days passed. The mural was taking shape; it would be an exciting feature once it was finished. Megan wondered whether her parents would come to Bronze Mountain as tourists one day, so that they could see the last piece that Tammy had conceived. She hoped that they would come, and she knew that if they did she would not accompany them.

Now and then she saw Larry. Twice she went out for dinner with him, and agonised in case Roan would walk into the restaurant with Petra. Larry was always

amusing, . but there were invitations which Megan
refused. It was becoming increasingly difficult to
pretend to be warm and relaxed with one man, when
with all her heart she wanted to be with another.

Roan she saw only occasionally. Always he avoided
her. It was as if he was taking no chances on having her
ask him to drive her again. Just as well he did not know
that once her mind was made up, not much would
change it.

The idea came to her quite suddenly. She was in the
resort store, choosing postcards to send home, when she
overheard him talking to one of the other engineers. He
did not see Megan, concealed behind the stand of
postcards, and when she realised what he was saying
she listened without shame. He was driving next day to
speak with a man called De Wet. The name was
unfamiliar to Megan, but that did not matter.

That evening Ann looked at her in dubious
amazement. 'Roan won't like it.'

'He'll be furious,' Megan agreed with a shaky laugh.

'Have you thought this all the way through?'

'If I did that I'd give up the whole idea.' Megan lifted
her head in a way that betokened challenge to the friend
who was getting to know her so well. 'I'll just take it
one step at a time.'

The first light of dawn tinged the eastern mountains
next morning when Megan concealed herself beside the
back seat of the jeep. Making herself as comfortable as
she could beneath an old tarpaulin, she wished her
hiding-place was a little roomier and more sweet-
smelling. And then she consoled herself with the
reflection that if her efforts today were successful her
discomfort would have been worth while.

About twenty minutes later Roan appeared. Megan
heard him open the boot of the car, felt the thud of a

case being deposited inside, then he got into the driver's seat, throwing a jacket on to the back seat at the same time.

He was whistling as he started the car and drove off. No problem there, Megan realised.

The road leading from Bronze Mountain was bumpy, and though Megan tried to cushion her head on a fold of the tarpaulin, she was glad when the car finally hit the main road. Comfortable she was not, but at least the bumping had stopped.

Roan seemed to drive with an easy confidence. There were many bends in the road, and he took them expertly, not with the slow hesitancy that might have been expected of a nervous driver. But while he was evidently relaxed and happy behind the wheel of the car, Megan wished she could say the same for herself. Had she been upright and able to look out of the window she might have enjoyed the drive; as it was, the winding road was beginning to make her feel sick. She tried to breathe slowly and steadily, and hoped she would not disgrace herself. One step at a time, she had told Ann—this was a step she had not anticipated.

Curse this car-sickness! She thought she had outgrown it years ago, why hadn't she realised that being buried beneath a pile of musty-smelling tarpaulin might bring it on again? Perhaps she could have taken some medicine to prevent it. Hindsight was always easy. The road had to improve, she told herself. Soon they would be out of the mountains, there would be no more bends, and she would be fine.

But the road grew worse. To the ever-increasing bends was added eventually another bumpy road, even bumpier than the first one. Megan pressed her hand over her mouth in despair.

The nausea increased. I'm going to die, she thought,

right here beneath this horrible tarpaulin, and Roan will never know what I went through for him.

Suddenly she gagged, and her breath came in a loud shudder.

In the front seat the whistling came to an abrupt stop as the car slid to a halt. 'What the devil!' Roan muttered, reaching behind him. His hand ran over the tarpaulin, stopping as it made contact with the form prone beneath it. The hand was still for a moment, and Megan, not daring to breathe, was still too.

A moment later he had jumped out of the car, opened the back door, and was pulling at the tarpaulin.

'Megan! My God, I should have known you'd never let up. You look terrible!'

She felt terrible, in more ways than one. She sat up, one hand still at her mouth, the other at her bruised back. Roan watched her silently for a moment, and then, as if he understood that she needed help, he pushed the tarpaulin aside and reached for her hand.

'What do you have to say for yourself?' he demanded when she had manouevred herself out of the car.

'I feel sick.'

The man she loved looked decidedly unsympathetic. 'Serve you right!'

Staggering to the edge of the road, she bent behind a bush a few moments. At last she came back to the car, walking on legs that were so weak that she thought she would fall. She did not look at Roan, was unaware that to him, at that moment, she was infinitely lovely and vulnerable, with her eyes huge and smudged in her ashen face, and her expression forlorn and a little childlike.

He put an arm around her shoulders and led her to a rock at the side of the road. 'You'd better sit down.'

She sank down on the ground and took a few deep

breaths. Fresh air had never been so sweet. 'You should deodorise your tarpaulin,' she muttered.

He gave a shout of laughter. 'Warn me next time you intend to stow away and I'll do just that. Megan, my darling Megan, what am I going to do with you now?'

'You could let me sit in front,' she said hopefully, wondering if the endearment meant he was not angry with her.

'I should lock you in the boot,' he told her unfeelingly.

'I'd feel better in front.'

'The thought of what could happen if I don't agree makes me squirm.' Suddenly he was laughing again. 'You're such an odd mixture, my Megan. One moment you're the most determined woman I ever met, the next you're a funny child with car-sickness.'

It was wonderful to hear him laugh—the most wonderful sound in all the world.

'Then you're not angry,' she said, relieved.

The amusement vanished. 'Yes, Megan.' His tone was quiet, and all the more chilling for it. 'I am angry.'

'You don't understand,' she pleaded.

'I'm not stupid. Who was it that told you that since the accident I don't drive with passengers? Larry?'

She swallowed. 'Ann.'

'In that case it was kindly meant,' he observed oddly. 'You decided that you would give me back my confidence, and having once made up your mind, nothing would stop you.'

He was so close to the truth. What could she say? Wordlessly she looked at him, and was only able to think how attractive he was. There was something very sensual in the firm set of his lips, in the gaunt cheekbones and the long strong jaw. Hard and masculine and sensual all at the same time.

Involuntarily she took a step towards him and saw his eyes glitter. He knew that she wanted to touch him, she thought, appalled.

'You really are a determined girl,' he commented.

'Determined meaning what?'

'Single-minded. Once you've made up your mind about something you proceed blithely and let nothing get in your way.'

'That's not so,' she protested hurt, though she knew there was in fact truth in what he said.

'No? You decided to finish what Tammy had begun. . . .'

'There was no harm in that, surely.'

After a moment, he said, 'No harm, no. But you set out for Bronze Mountain without even waiting to find out what had happened to the wall. It was months later, the mural could have been finished.'

'But Tammy had left no sketches. I was the only one who knew what she'd planned.'

'Another artist might have had the existing work erased, and designed something entirely different.'

'Yes,' Megan acknowledged, and wondered why she had not thought of that possibility when she had made the original decision.

'You decided you would get me to drive you,' Roan went on relentlessly. 'No matter what my own feelings happened to be.'

She eyed him uncertainly. 'There was always a reason.'

'Of course.' His lips tilted mockingly. 'The ducklings. Your supplies.'

Megan curled her fingers into her palms. 'You didn't believe me?'

There was a glimmer of humour in his eyes. 'Should I have?'

Defiantly she lifted her chin. 'Yes!'

'What ever else I may be, Megan, I'm not naïve.'

She felt her cheeks grow warm. 'I know that.' She was quiet a moment, wishing that she had more control over the conversation. 'I know you've never wanted to drive me.'

His mouth was hard, and over the gaunt cheekbones the flesh was stretched taut. 'That's not entirely true. On your first day at Bronze Mountain I asked you to have dinner with me. I offered to drive you to the station next day to fetch your luggage.'

'Ann said that was odd. Oh!' Megan clapped a hand to her mouth. 'I shouldn't have said that.'

Something flickered in his eyes. 'It's all right. I know you've discussed me.' He looked down at her a long moment, but she could not read his expression. 'You refused me on both scores.'

'Yes. . . .' How very well she remembered the evening. She could see herself looking into the canyon, embarrassed at Roan's questions, angry at him because he was Brendon Stevens, a callous man who had not cared enough to write a personal letter or pay Tammy's family a visit. If only the evening could be wiped from memory. But life wasn't like that; the slate could not be wiped clean.

But there *could* be a new start. With some bending and some compromise on both sides, there could always be a new start. She was about to put the thought into words when Roan spoke into the silence.

'You didn't trust me enough to come with me then.'

'I trust you now,' she said simply, looking up at him, aware that her heart was in her eyes.

After another long moment he said, 'I'm glad.' And she had a feeling that he wasn't glad at all.

'I'm sorry about that first night, I wish I could say

more than that.' Her throat was dry. 'Why did you want to drive me then, Roan?'

'I had my reasons.' His tone was short. 'A question of my own, Megan. Why did you stow away?'

There was something unnerving in the way he was looking at her. He was too near her—and yet not near enough. His eyes were on her face, studying her with an intensity that made her tremble. And she wanted nothing so much as to be in his arms.

'Why did I stow away?' she whispered, playing for time.

He made an impatient sound in his throat, and it came to Megan that if Roan had doubts about his driving, he did not doubt himself on anything else. This man had no weaknesses. He was strong and arrogant and sure of himself—too sure of himself, she decided ruefully.

'Never mind, we both know the real reason. And as she stared at him, 'Don't bat those innocent eyes at me, Megan, it won't get you anywhere. What excuse were you going to give me?'

Suddenly she felt incredibly foolish. 'I need supplies—paint and some new brushes. I really did mean to get them, Roan.'

'In that case,' he said lazily, 'you're on a wasted journey. You won't buy them where we're going.'

Something in his tone set a quiver of apprehension shivering along her spine. 'Where *are* we going?'

'Off the beaten track. To a game park.'

She stared at him incredulously. 'A game park!'

'And I think you may find,' he said very softly, 'that impetuousness has its own dangers.'

Her heart thudded crazily against her rib-cage. 'I know you wouldn't hurt me,' she said bumpily.

'What I have in mind doesn't hurt,' he murmured.

She knew he was going to kiss her even before he reached for her. Her body was alive with the need for him, she could not have pushed him away. Not that she tried. Somewhere was the knowledge that she should not make it too easy for him, that he should not know quite how much she wanted him, for if he did his power over her would be absolute.

But she was quite still as his head descended and his arms closed around her. His mouth found hers, and as he kissed her, lightly, tenderly, over the clamouring of her pulses came the thought, this is like the first time. All the weeks in between have been wiped out and we really can make a fresh start.

The pressure of his lips increased. Now he was kissing her hungrily, as if he had been waiting a long time for this moment. His arms tightened, then he was pressing her to him, moulding her soft body against his long hard one. All thought of passiveness fled Megan's mind as she was consumed with the wonder and excitement of what was happening. Without reserve she kissed him back, glorying in the feel of his lips on hers.

And then his hands began to move over her, exploring her shoulders and her throat, sliding down to her waist, shaping themselves to the soft curve of her hips. One hand pushed up her blouse, slid beneath it, and for a moment lay palm-down and motionless against the bare skin. The contact sent a sharp flame of desire shooting through her, and she wound her arms around his neck, mindlessly pressing herself closer against him as her fingers revelled in the glossy thickness of his hair.

She was not thinking now. It did not matter if he knew how she felt about him. There was only the silence of the veld, and the rough scrub against her legs, and the vibrant man's body against every inch of her own.

When his head lifted and his arms loosened their hold, she felt dazed. 'This was rather more than I had in mind. I'm sorry,' she heard him say.

He was concerned about her, remorseful because he had forced his attentions on her, and she was touched. Surely Roan had understood the nature of her response.

'That's all right,' she said softly. 'I suppose I asked for it.'

'You did. But actually I was thinking of myself.'

Megan's breath caught in her throat as she jerked her head up to look at him. Beneath his tan he was pale, and his eyes had the familiar bleakness she was beginning to recognise.

'You really are angry with me?' she said uncertainly.

'Yes.'

She struggled with herself. 'I could go back.'

'On foot?' He gave a mirthless laugh. 'Unfortunately it's impossible. No, my impetuous Megan, whether we turn back or go farther, either way I'll have to take you with me.'

Now that the sexual desire was beginning to subside inside her she was able to focus on him properly. He was six feet and two inches of tension. From his face to his muscle-bunched throat and shoulders, to the legs that were too firmly planted on the rough ground, there was tension.

What have I done? Megan asked herself, as her heart went out to him.

'Then you won't take me back to Bronze Mountain?' she said aloud.

'We've gone this far, we'll go on.' His tone was clipped. Mockingly he added, 'Too bad about your supplies, they'll have to wait for another day—and another driver.'

'Does it bother you so much to drive me?' she asked gently.

'A pointless question at this stage. You've left me no choice.'

'I thought I was doing the right thing,' she said unhappily.

'Did you really?' He took a step towards her and gripped her shoulders as he had done before when he'd been under stress. 'Did you really, Megan? Or are you just one of those people who like to meddle in other people's lives?'

She flinched. 'You know that's not true!'

The eyes that looked down at her were decidedly frosty. 'You've been at me ever since you found out I was in hospital.'

'Only because I thought it was necessary.'

'I've no time for meddlers.'

She decided to ignore the barb. 'You're a good driver, Roan.'

'And you, I suppose, are an expert on the subject.'

It was not easy to remain calm. 'You forget, you drove quite a way before you realised I was there. You're. . . .' She paused, groping for words. 'You're so in control of yourself, of the road. Some of those bends were hairpin.' She made a rueful mouth. 'I ought to know!'

Either the humour was lost on him, or the timing was bad. 'I don't need you to tell me I'm a good driver.'

'Because you know it anyway.' She looked at him. 'You just don't want passengers?'

'I suggest we drop this conversation.'

'When will you want passengers?' she persisted, hating herself for what she was doing to him, knowing that she was risking his anger, and yet realising that she might never get the chance to pin him down on this topic again.

'When I'm ready,' he answered her curtly.

'When will that be, Roan?'

His eyes met hers, then shifted away. 'Perhaps never.'

'You don't mean that. You can't!' She put her hand on his arm, and felt it grow instantly rigid. It was as if the passionate love scene of a few minutes ago had never taken place. 'What happened was an accident,' she reasoned with him—pleaded with him.

'Can you leave it alone, Megan!'

'I want to help you.'

'Single-minded as I said.' A wintry smile crossed his face. 'Get back in the car.'

'Please try to understand,' she pleaded.

'Get back in the car. Now!'

CHAPTER SEVEN

MEGAN sat in the front seat beside Roan as they drove on. She should have felt better, but she did not. The physical discomfort was gone, now that she could see the bends in the road before the car came to them she was no longer car-sick. But in every other way she felt worse. At least, while she had lain concealed beneath the ill-smelling tarpaulin there had been the feeling that she was on the way to achieving her objective. There had been a feeling of anticipation, of hope. There had been the consoling knowledge that her stomach was queasy in good cause.

Now she knew differently. Roan did not want her help. He balked at every attempt she made. Single-minded, he had called her, and though there had been a slight humour in the way he had said the words, there had been no humour in his meaning. He resented the fact that she was with him.

When the hairpin bends had his attention she was able to look at him. His face was still pale, and what she could see of his profile was taut. The hands on the wheel were white-knuckled. He drove as well as before, negotiating the difficult road expertly. But something was missing. He no longer whistled. There was no sense of ease. Roan was an excellent driver, but with a passenger beside him he was unhappy.

It was silent in the car. Megan would have liked to talk, but the few topics that came to mind all appeared totally out of place. As for Roan, it seemed he had no wish to make conversation.

Unhappily she turned to the window. Normally she would have been enchanted by the grandeur of the countryside, but now it was lost on her. Only dimly did she register the unfolding vistas of mountains and forests, the pine-clad slopes and the waterfalls slipping down mossy cliffs. So busy was she with her thoughts that she hardly noticed when they came into farmlands: tobacco farms where the leaves were lush and darkly green, and then citrus orchards, where oranges and lemons and grapefruit hung heavy on trees whose stumps were painted white to ward off disease.

It was only when the scenery began to change once more that Megan sat up and took note of her surroundings. The neat farmlands were behind them now, and they were driving through bushveld. Untamed veld, windswept and sparsely treed. Rough country this, and yet with a haunting quality that had a beauty of its own.

She looked at Roan. 'We're there?'

He did not turn his eyes from the road. 'Almost.'

He was still tense, a tension that communicated itself to Megan. But now she was also excited. Once, many years ago, the family had visited a game park. A memory came to mind. It had been very hot and they had been driving for almost an hour without spotting any game. At a river they had stopped, and Tammy, bored and restless, had wanted to get out of the car and go to the water. 'For heaven's sake, you could be eaten alive!' their mother had shouted in panic, and Megan, a mature twelve-year-old against Tammy's nine, had reached across her sister to close the door and say, 'Idiot!' Not five minutes later a lion had walked out of the bush.

'You've been to a game park?' Roan asked into her musings. They were the first words he had spoken for more than an hour.

'Once. Tammy wanted to get out of the car and didn't know a lion was near by. At the last moment. . . .' She paused. 'It was a long time ago.'

'I can imagine.' Roan's profile was grim, and as she saw his hands tighten on the wheel Megan was instantly sorry she had mentioned her sister. The few words of talk had been a relief; now, it seemed, Roan meant to withdraw from her again.

Determined not to let that happen, she said, 'You haven't told me where we're going.'

'I thought I had.'

'Only vaguely. A game park, that's all I know. The Kruger National Park?'

He shook his head. 'A private park. Its name is Shengala.'

Concealing her surprise, knowing only that she could not let the conversation die, Megan persisted. 'You're going to visit someone there?'

'Right.' He paused, and Megan wondered whether she would have to ask more questions. But he went on, 'Not a social visit. There are things I want to see at Shengala.'

'Animals?'

For the first time since their roadside stop he grinned. 'Any game we see will be a bonus. No, Megan, I'm going to observe, to take notes. I'll be needing them for my next project.'

Abstractedly she registered the fact that when he smiled there was a cleft that ran from his eyes to the corners of his mouth. There must have been a time when Roan had smiled often.

'You're going to start a game park of your own?' she asked.

'I'd like to.' His voice altered, lost the hardness that had become too familiar, became almost introspective. 'It's a dream I've had for some time.'

'You'll start it when Bronze Mountain is finished?'

'I plan to.' Momentarily he turned his eyes from the road. 'I take it you know my real status at Bronze Mountain?' And when she nodded, 'Ann again. She must trust you, I know she's not one for idle gossip. Yes, Megan, a game park has been on the cards for almost a year now.'

'Even before the accident?'

As if he guessed at her thoughts, he said, 'I'd hoped to be at the planning stage before now.' He shrugged.

'Tell me about it,' Megan invited. 'Will it be like the Kruger National Park?' The game park she named was famous far beyond the boundaries of Southern Africa, and could not be far from here.

He laughed, the sound reaching to her in a way which made her want to put out her hand and touch him—a gesture Roan might not appreciate. She forced herself to sit very still.

'Now that would be ambitious. Too big for one man. No, more like Shengala. You'll see that park for yourself. Though mine will have some special features of its own.'

Even without seeing Roan's game park—there was no way she could see it, for after she left Bronze Mountain she would not see Roan again—she knew that his project would be unique. She had only to think of Bronze Mountain, with its attractive layout and its diverse amenities, to know that.

'Shengala's around the next bend,' she heard him say.

Enchanted eyes took in a pair of huge stone gates. On each side was a flame tree heavy with coral flowers. Just beside the gates was a signboard with the head of a giraffe painted on it, and the name Shengala in bold white letters.

They had not been in the park long when Roan stopped the car so that Megan could watch a herd of impala. The dainty-looking deer were grazing in a clearing; only one of their number, a stag with sharp curving horns, stood a little to one side, alert for danger from predators.

A little further on Roan exclaimed under his breath as he applied his brakes. 'What is it . . .?' Megan began, and then excitement welled inside her as she saw a herd of zebra, their black-and-white striped bodies magnificent. Not far away grazed a group of wildebeeste, the bison-like animals unkempt and surly-looking.

'Like old men who forgot to brush their hair this morning,' said Megan, and drew a rare smile from Roan.

'Isn't it strange,' he observed, still with that wonderful smile, 'that two such unlikely animals are usually to be found together.'

'You love animals?' she asked as they drove farther.

'There was a time when I wanted to be a game warden.'

But he'd gone on to become an entrepreneur instead. Only someone with much money would be able to own and develop holiday resorts.

'You said developing a game park had always been a dream. Just a sideline to your other interests, Roan?'

'Not a sideline at all. I expect it to be a profitable venture. Even my pet projects have to pay their way.'

He was quite a man, Megan thought, when they eventually drove further. No stranger, unaware of his personal trauma, would see him as anything but highly successful. A man above all other men, radiating an aura of strength and power along with a potent sexuality.

They stopped again, this time to watch a kudu

nibbling leaves from a tree with disdainful dignity. 'Gorgeous!' Megan exclaimed.

'It is,' Roan agreed. On a new note he continued, 'Bring any luggage with you?'

She stared at him. 'Of course not.'

'No standard stowaway gear?' His voice was lazily insolent. And as a quiver of apprehension tingled suddenly inside her, he went on, 'Do you normally sleep nude or in a nightgown?'

The breath skittered in her throat. 'What do you mean?'

'I only wondered how you were going to manage tonight?'

It was impossible to conceal her trembling. 'As I've done for the past weeks—in the cabin at Bronze Mountain.'

'No, my dear.' His eyes mocked her. 'In a room at Shengala.'

'That's impossible!' she burst out.

'It's a fact.'

'Ann will be concerned.'

'That's something you should have thought about when you decided to force yourself on me.'

'I didn't know. I didn't think. . . .' Megan bit her lip.
'That's how you think of it, isn't it, that I forced myself on to you?'

'Didn't you?' he responded lightly. 'Our host will be Dave De Wet, an old friend of mine.'

'Won't he be surprised when he knows . . . when he finds out . . .?'

'That you stowed away? I think we'll leave out that part, don't you?'

'He won't be surprised that I'll be here overnight?'

An eyebrow lifted negligently. 'I doubt it.'

'Men of the world,' the gesture and the tone seemed

to say, 'understand these situations. Besides, it's not the first time I've travelled with a woman.'

I should be worried about tonight, Megan told herself. And all I can think about is the other women Dave has seen with Roan. What's happened to me in the last weeks? Have I gone mad? I don't know myself any more.

'There must be a way of getting back to Bronze Mountain tonight,' she said dully. 'It only took a few hours to get here.'

'I've things to see and to do here at Shengala. I won't be through in a day. Look, Megan, there's the kudu's mate.'

Sure enough a second kudu was emerging through the trees, the female this time, without the lovely horns of the male, but still quite beautiful. Daintily she stepped through the long grass, turning once to survey the occupants of the car, her eyes big and liquid-looking.

I should be thrilled at the sight, Megan told herself, and all I can think of is that I must spend at least another day in Roan's company.

They drove on at last, and she kept her eyes firmly on the bush beyond her window just as if she was determined not to miss an animal that might be hidden there. In fact, her mind was not on animals at all. She could only think of the man at her side. She was intensely aware of him just inches away from her. She was aware too of a tingling in the air. Was it possible that air could be charged with sexual tension? she wondered wildly. It was a strange sensation, unsettling and at the same time almost unbearably exciting. Did Roan feel it too? Could he be unaware of it? Megan did not think so.

They came at last to the rest camp at Shengala, and

she was relieved. What the next hours would hold she did not know, but at least, temporarily, there would be a respite from a tension which she found herself less and less able to cope with.

By comparison with the rest camps in the Kruger National Park, this one was small, she saw at a glance. Small but very pretty. Bordering a lush lawn was a circle of rondawels, each of the round huts having a thatched roof and tropical creepers climbing white-washed walls. Outside them stood barbecue stands with coal and wood piled ready for the evening braaivleis. And everywhere were more of the flame trees which Megan had seen at the gates of Shengala.

As Roan drew up beside a bigger hut with a sign that said 'Office', a tall man came out to greet them. His face was deeply tanned, as if he spent most of his days out of doors, and his smile was attractive. Roan got out of the car and the two men clasped hands. Then Roan had opened the door for Megan—an unexpected courtesy from someone who had been so lazily insolent just a short while ago—and he was introducing her to Dave.

'Megan, this is Dave De Wet. Dave, I want you to meet a friend of mine, Megan Westcott. She thought she'd like to see Shengala.'

So simply done. With the ease of a man who had had to make explanations for many women in his time. The knowledge that there had been women in Roan's life always hurt. Foolishly, since there was not even the possibility that Megan herself could ever have a place in his life.

But the hurt was concealed behind a smile as she clasped the big out-reached hand, and responded to Dave's 'Glad to have you here, Megan,' with an 'I'm glad too,' of her own.

'I bet you folks would like something cool to drink before we get down to anything,' said Dave. 'You have to see my new patio area, Roan.'

'That's what I'm here for.' An easy grin warmed the rugged face, and Megan wondered why he could be so relaxed with everyone but herself.

The patio was a long slastoed slab in front of a small restaurant. Wide and cool and sheltered from sun and rain by a bright awning, it was furnished with chairs and tables of white cane, and adorned with big pots of azaleas and gardenias. 'Very nice,' Roan commented approvingly. 'And in just the right place.'

The patio was in a high spot that overlooked the river. As Megan sipped chilled orange juice from a long fluted glass, she let her eyes go to the river bank. The sand was criss-crossed with the hoof-marks of many animals, and even as she watched some impala emerged from the bush and came daintily to the water.

'See the hippos?' Roan interrupted his conversation with Dave to ask.

'No. . . .' She searched the river.

'There. Look where my finger is pointing.'

'Oh!' she gasped, for now she did see them. Dark humps in the water, almost submerged and motionless— she had taken them for rocks. Then one of the humps moved, surfaced, a mouth opened wide and a shower of bubbles rippled across the water.

Megan laughed, the sound high and joyous on the silent air. She turned to the men and saw them watching her, Dave a little speculatively, Roan with an expression that sent her pulses unaccountably racing. The laughter died abruptly in her throat, and she turned back to the water, and now she did not find the water-blowing hippo amusing. Her cheeks were warm, and she could think only of Roan.

Drinks finished, the men proceeded to more serious conversation, and Megan elected to explore the camp on her own. There was so much to see, and she liked all of it. Shengala had been designed with an abundance of taste. Visitors to the little game park would enjoy themselves here.

Standing at the fence and looking across the bush, Megan wondered about the park that Roan would develop. It would have Shengala's good points and more. She had only to think of Bronze Mountain to know that whatever Roan turned his energies to would be superb.

But Roan's game park was one that she would never see. She would finish the mural at Bronze Mountain, and then she would leave the Lowveld and never return to it, for if she did there would always be the chance that she might run into Roan. Even if she did not meet him, there would be memories to haunt her anew, so that a part of her would always be lingering for something she could never have.

She was still at the fence when Roan found her and called her for lunch. The meal was light, ice-cream and a fruit salad which was a glorious combination of mangoes and lychees and the soft pulp of grenadillas.

After that it was time to go for a drive. They went in Dave's jeep this time, for Dave knew all the best spots at Shengala. Megan sat between the two men on the front seat. Both male bodies were equally close to hers, but she was aware only of Roan. Though Dave could not help moving against her as he drove, it was Roan who caused her anguish. He was wearing shorts. Try as she would, she could not seem to stop her eyes from straying to the long legs and thighs. She could feel every inch of the leg that lay against hers, could feel the way her skin burned to its touch. Though she was wearing jeans, she might as well have been wearing nothing at all for the effect Roan's closeness had on her.

She sat very still, trying to stifle the quivering that seized her body. A pulse was beating in her leg, in a spot where she had never felt a pulse before. And she hoped, quite desperately, that Roan did not feel it too.

Water, it seemed, was plentiful at Shengala, for there was lots of game. Dave drove very slowly, pointing, talking, explaining. Once he stopped to let them admire a few giraffe. Even through her tension Megan could not help being fascinated. Two adult giraffe were nibbling leaves from the tops of some tall acacias, and as the car drew up alongside them, they turned aloof and dignified heads. A few yards away were three smaller giraffe, much smaller, babies. No dignity there, Megan thought amused, as she watched them lope through the trees on awkward and unsteady legs.

'Later perhaps you'll see giraffe drink,' said Dave, registering her amusement. 'Now there's a sight that's worth seeing.'

He drove on, but though there was often game to be seen near the road, he stopped only rarely. This was not meant to be a pleasure trip. Roan's purpose in coming to Shengala was to learn. The two men discussed roads and the culling of animals. Above all else they discussed water. Dave drove right past a group of warthogs waddling comically through the bush, only to stop at a windmill where Roan was absorbed in discovering why it had been placed in that particular position.

And then it was on again, this time to stop at the river. Dave's jeep could negotiate the bush, and he left the road and pushed over the scrub to a point where there was a wonderful view of the water. Zebra were drinking near at hand, and a little farther was a giraffe.

'Look, Megan,' Roan pointed, and she watched

amused as the giraffe straddled long front legs so that
its neck could reach the water. As Dave had said, it was
a sight worth seeing.

The men watched too, but only for a few moments.
Then they were talking again, discussing the necessity of
having enough water to attract game. Megan let the
talk wash over her. She was watching the animals, but
even the novelty of seeing them in their wild state was
only on the periphery of her mind. The day was passing
quickly. Already afternoon shadows were beginning to
spread along the sandy banks of the river and over the
scrub beneath the thorny acacias. Soon it would be
dark, and with night would come a set of problems she
had not anticipated when she had hidden in Roan's car
this morning.

Nothing had been said so far about a room, and Megan
wondered whether Dave assumed she was Roan's
girl-friend, and that they would be sharing a room. A
natural misunderstanding in the circumstances, but Roan
would put him right. She was worrying needlessly.

Just as Roan said, 'Elephant,' her eye was caught by
a waving curve of grey above an acacia. Excitement
gripped Megan, so much so that she even forgot Roan
and her dilemma. The two men stopped their
conversation as a large shape lumbered through the
bushes, its trunk curling around the slender stem of a
tree, breaking it just as easily as Megan might have
broken a match. Emerging on the sandy bank, the
elephant paused and looked around. The great ears
flapped backwards, and the trunk rose as the mouth
opened to emit a bellow that echoed across the veld.
Then the elephant dipped its trunk in the river, lifted it
out, and splashed water over its dusty hide.

'Wonderful!' Megan breathed. 'I could watch this for
hours!'

'I could too,' said Dave, 'but it's time to go back.'

It was almost dark by the time they reached camp. A guard stood at the gates, ready to close them just before sunset merged into night. Megan had seen the camp restaurant, but perhaps it was only seldom used, for outside most rondawels fires had been lit, and the smells and sounds of the braaivleis filled the air. Whether it was Dave's custom to have a braaivleis she did not know, but he had organised one for tonight, and invited Roan and Megan to join him. The fire must have been lit some time ago, for the coals were already grey, the flames had died and the smoky heat that rose to the iron grid was ideal for cooking meat. Megan watched as Dave put thick pieces of steak and boerewors on to braai.

'So much!' she exclaimed feelingly. 'We'll never eat all that.'

'Want to bet?' Dave laughed, and Roan, laughing too, observed, 'Haven't you learned yet what fresh air does to one's appetite?'

The laughter lessened the tension that had been with her since they had left the river-bank. Things would sort themselves out, they had to.

In the west the sky was brilliant with the last colours of sunset. The colours faded, and as is common in Africa, where the sunset is spectacular but brief, suddenly it was dark.

They ate in the dark, with a kerosene lamp casting light on their food. In the rondawels there was electric light, but for outdoor eating Dave preferred a more rustic atmosphere. The steak was soft, the boerewors spicy, and the hot buttered mealies were hard to resist, even though Megan felt she had eaten more than ever in her life before. There was wine, a bubbling Cape Riesling, and she leaned back, feeling mellow and content.

When the meat had been eaten Dave put more wood on the fire. The flames leaped, and Megan saw the faces of the men, Dave's lean and good-natured, Roan's rugged yet softened, and as always she felt something turn over inside her at sight of him. He was sitting beside her, his deck-chair so close to hers that she could have reached out and touched him. She would have to remember him like this, with his face softened in the firelight, his pipe in his mouth, long legs outstretched. That was all she could ever have of Roan—memories. She would zealously cherish the happy ones.

After a while the fire began to die, and Roan said, 'You're cold.'

'A little,' she admitted.

'Didn't think to bring anything with you?' he asked as he pushed his chair even closer to hers and put an arm around her shoulders, drawing her to him.

'. . . No.'

'Tough,' he murmured against her ear.

'You're cold, Megan?' asked Dave. 'Don't you have a warm sweater with you?'

'Some women are unpredictable when they pack.' Roan was so close to her that she could hear the bubble of laughter in his throat.

'I'll put another log on the fire,' Dave suggested.

'It's late,' said Roan. 'Time to turn in, I think.'

Megan still did not know where she would sleep. She supposed that Dave would show her to her room now. But he said, 'Right, folks, it's goodnight, then. See you both in the morning.'

Megan watched disbelievingly as he turned in the direction of his rondawel. She had been so sure that he would first show her to her own quarters.

'Come on,' said Roan, cupping her elbow with his hand.

'*You're* going to show me to my room?'

Again he laughed, the sound low and disturbingly seductive in the sweet-smelling bushveld night. 'Of course.'

It was very dark now. Outside the rondawels all the fires had burned low, and few lights shone in the windows. People who intended to leave camp at dawn, the best time to see animals, had already retired to bed.

Megan did not fear the dark. But this was no ordinary darkness. The path on which they walked was not far from the fence, and there was something extraordinarily exciting in the knowledge that only yards from where they were there might be animals. In Africa at night there is always the sound of the crickets, a high unrelenting shrilling. But in the game park there were other sounds too—scufflings in the high grass beyond the fence, evidence of invisible animals, the eerie laugh of a hyena, the roar of a lion, rolling and echoing over the silent land. And then, suddenly, the trumpeting of an elephant.

'Our elephant?' Megan wondered aloud.

'Could be,' Roan answered her softly, and she knew he was thinking, as she was, of the great grey beast that had splashed water over itself at the river. *Our* elephant. There was a curious intimacy in the word 'our.'

Megan was always aware of Roan when he was near her. As he walked by her side now, hand on her arm, guiding her in the dark, she was more aware of him than ever. There was something very thrilling about walking through the dark camp compound with Roan. One more memory. She would never forget the cool bushveld night and the sounds of the animals, the trumpeting of the elephant and the roar of the lion. And the man, so close to her that she could sense every muscle in the long thigh that brushed her as they walked.

If she could have prolonged the walk she would have done so. But they were approaching a rondawel, and Roan had taken a key from his pocket.

'This is it?'

'This is it.' His tone was oddly enigmatic.

She watched him unlock the door. She could have done it herself, but if he wanted to be gallant she would be churlish to refuse him the pleasure.

'See you in the morning.' When Roan had opened the door, she echoed Dave's earlier words. 'Goodnight.'

'You can say that when you've brushed your teeth.'

About to step past him into the rondawel, she stared at him. 'My teeth! Heavens, I don't have a toothbrush.'

'Isn't it a good thing that I had the foresight to get you one at the camp store?' he said mockingly.

'Thank you.' Relieved, she put out her hand. 'Please give it to me.'

'When we're inside.'

'Inside?' Adrenalin pumped suddenly and rapidly through her system. 'You're not coming inside!'

'We both know that I am. Are you going to go in, Megan, or are you going to leave the door open so that the insects can get in too?'

Insects? Roan was the danger, not the few insects that might be attracted by the open door and the small light shining inside.

'You can't mean ... that we're sharing this place?' she asked shakily.

'You sound so innocent.' His voice had changed. 'Almost as if. . . .' He stopped, and when he went on his voice had hardened. 'You must have known we might be sharing.'

CHAPTER EIGHT

HAD she known? She had rationalised that even if Dave had thought she was Roan's girl-friend—mistress?—Roan would have disillusioned him and insisted on separate sleeping quarters. Yet in some part of her mind perhaps she *had* known that they would be sharing a rondawel.

'It's impossible,' she got out.

'That's something we can discuss inside—before we're overrun by mosquitoes. Well, Megan, are you going to move?' As she continued to stare at him, he scooped her suddenly into his arms and carried her through the open door.

He kicked the door closed with his foot. She thought he would put her down, but instead he continued to hold her. One arm was beneath her knees, and her head was cradled against his chest, and when she looked up she saw that he was looking down at her. A table-light cast a glow over the room, but it was not so bright that she could see his eyes. She could only make out the long line of the jaw and the muscle that moved suddenly in his throat. Her own throat was dry and she could feel the blood pounding in her temples.

'Brides get carried over thresholds.' The words were out before she had known she would say them. She didn't even know why she'd said them. Nervousness, perhaps.

His tone was suddenly harsh. 'You're not a bride, Megan, and I'm no bridegroom.' So saying, he set her abruptly down on the floor and moved away from her.

The mood—there had been a mood, surely, however brief it had been—was shattered. She was glad, she told herself, for there was no knowing quite where it might have led them. She knew she was also disappointed.

Megan was trembling as she took in the interior of the rondawel. The simple furnishings were tasteful, the colours cool, so that a guest might feel relaxed even on the hottest days. In normal circumstances it was a room which would have appealed to her artistic nature.

But the circumstances were anything but normal. Not for Megan. She could only look at the double bed that stood on one side of the room—dominating the room, so it seemed. Her eyes were held by it as if magnetised.

It was some moments before she could trust herself to look at Roan. 'There must be some other way.'

He had not moved since he had put her down and taken a few steps away from her. Turning to him now, she saw that he had been watching her. The skin was stretched tight over his cheekbones, and his expression was mocking. 'Afraid not,' he said flatly.

'There's only one bed,' she said unhappily.

'The vulnerable virgin!' His tone was harsh.

Megan flinched. 'You make virginity sound like something to apologise for!'

'If you are in fact a virgin.'

She looked up at him. 'I think you know I am,' she said simply. 'At the vlei—that first day—you thought I was.'

'I could have been wrong.'

'Don't you believe me?' she asked, a little desperately, wishing he would speak.

His eyes swept her face, lingering on unsteady lips, moving to her throat, then upwards once more, to meet her eyes this time. 'Perhaps,' he replied at last.

'Then you can see how impossible it is that we should share a room.'

Roan came towards her quite suddenly, one long hand capturing her chin, turning it upwards. The other hand went to the back of her neck, the fingers sliding up beneath her hair. She could not move away from him. Even her eyes were no longer her own, for she found that she could not move them from his.

'There comes a time when girls lose their virginity,' Roan said softly.

Megan swallowed hard. 'This isn't the time.'

'Does the idea of making love with me revolt you so much?'

It doesn't revolt me at all. I want you to make love to me. But not for the wrong reasons. Not because I'm an available female, because through my own stupidity we've been forced into a situation of intimacy. I want you to make love to me—because you love me.

There! She had admitted it to herself.

To him she could say only, 'I don't want to discuss it. Ask Dave for another room.'

'There isn't one.'

'Roan. . . .'

He made an impatient sound in his throat. 'My God, Megan, couldn't you have foreseen something like this happening when you decided to stow away in my car?'

'No. I didn't think. . . .'

'Well, that's a pity,' he said dangerously, 'because if you remember, I told you that stowaways have to accept the circumstances of their actions.'

In the moment before he pulled her against him she knew what would happen. Knew too that she wanted it. The first kiss was hard, hungry, a man's response to a situation that was not of his own making. It was a kiss that lasted only a few seconds, and then Roan lifted his head, and Megan heard the ragged intake of his breath.

When he kissed her again there was a difference.

As if he wanted to leave her lips for last, his mouth began to trace a path across her face. A light sensual path that started around the corners of her eyes and moved downwards, hovering tantalisingly around the corners of her lips before moving to her ears, lingering there to tease at one lobe before travelling to the other, then going down to her throat, finding places that Megan, till that moment, had never known were sensitive.

And then his mouth found hers. The lightness was gone now. His mouth was hard and possessive, staking a claim which Megan ached to give him. He did not have to force her lips open, they opened voluntarily to his as he kissed her, deeply, thirstily, as if he could never have enough. Her fingers found the hair at the back of his head, knotted themselves in it, and as he pressed her body against his her hands jerked convulsively, and then she was yielding to him, letting her soft curves be moulded against his hard ones.

She felt his hands at her shirt, opening the buttons, sliding it from her shoulders, and she made no effort to resist him. As his hands went to her breasts, cupping them, caressing them, letting her nipples harden into his fingers, she felt the blood singing in her veins. She knew suddenly that she had been waiting all night for this moment. All her life, perhaps.

Imperceptibly they were moving closer to the bed. Megan gave a little gasp when she felt it against the back of her thighs. But she was not frightened. She loved Roan. And though she had always thought that she would sleep with a man only when she was married to him, she knew, quite certainly, that what would happen now would be beautiful.

He began to undress her, and she had not known that he was capable of such an agonising tenderness. And then he was holding her again, lifting her into his arms and putting her down on the bed.

He was about to lie down himself when a roar rent the night. A lion—and near by. For the past minutes Megan had had no sense of reality, of time or place. Save for Roan nothing existed. Now, as she thrilled to the primitiveness of the lion's roar, she remembered where she was.

'What would Dave say if he could see us now?' she wondered aloud.

'I don't think he'd be surprised.' Roan actually sounded amused.

She looked at him startled. 'You don't?'

He shrugged, the wide shoulders powerful in the dim light. 'A man and a woman, alone in a small rondawel, with just one bed. Do *you* think he'd be surprised?'

The words hit her with the shock of an icy jet of water. A double bed. A man and a woman, alone. Any man, any woman. They were only doing what Dave would have expected them to do. What Roan would have done just as easily with any other woman.

He was lowering himself on to the bed, reaching for her as he did so, when she shrank away from him. 'No!'

He looked puzzled. 'Megan?'

'Don't touch me!'

'I don't understand.'

'I'm the one who didn't understand. I do now.' She looked about for something to cover herself with, and seeing nothing—her clothes were on the floor beyond her reach—she folded her arms about her bare breasts. 'I fell into your trap.'

'You're crazy!'

'I was.' She felt very cold. 'You said as a stowaway I'd have to abide by your terms.'

'Don't go on, Megan.' He was standing now, tall and powerful beside the bed, and his face had taken on an ominous expression.

'You said there was only one rondawel.'

'It's true.'

'I don't believe you. I don't remember hearing you ask Dave for another one.'

'Shengala happens to be full.'

'I've only your word for it.' She shifted her eyes away from him, keeping them firmly on the farthest wall of the room, because it hurt so much to look at him. She loved him, but to be made love to by him merely because she was an available woman would be to cheapen both her feelings and her memories.

'Right. You've only my word.' Roan's tone was chilling. 'Get beneath the sheets, Megan.'

The order had her spinning round to look at him.

'You're quite safe from me. I won't touch you. But get between the sheets. I happen to be a normal man with normal instincts.'

There it was again. A normal man, alone with a woman. Any woman.

'Where will you sleep?' she asked jerkily, a few moments later, when she lay with the sheet pulled up to her chin.

His only answer was to pull two chairs together. His movements were deliberate and controlled. She saw him unbuckle his belt, and she wrenched her eyes away from him once more. Lying very still, trying to make her breathing slow and steady, she kept her eyes on the same dim wall as before. Tears were gathering beneath her eyelids, and she was trying very hard to keep them from falling. One tear escaped on to her cheek, and though her impulse was to dash it away, she kept her hand firmly by her side. She would *not* let Roan see that she was crying.

It did not take him long to get ready. Presently she heard him stretch out on the chairs, muttering once beneath his breath because their distance from each other was not correct. She heard the chairs shift, then all was still.

If Roan slept, Megan did not. She did not know how long she lay awake. Her ears were filled with the sound of the steady breathing inside the room, and the cries of the animals outside. Once more a lion roared, and she knew how different things would have been if the first roar had never sounded. She would have given herself to Roan, gladly, lovingly. And she would never have known that the act meant no more to him than normal physical gratification.

Would I have been happier that way, fulfilled yet ignorant? Megan asked herself in the darkness. She fell asleep without knowing the answer.

For a few moments, when Megan awoke, she did not know where she was. And then the events of the previous day came rushing back to her, and her cheeks grew hot with memory. Beneath the sheets she was naked. Roan had taken off her shirt, and some time during the night she herself had discarded her jeans, not wishing them to be creased the next morning, as these were the only clothes she had with her.

Holding the sheet carefully to her chin, she sat up and looked around her. The chairs which Roan had used for a bed had been pushed back into their usual places, and the rondawel was empty. At least she was spared the embarrassment of wondering how she would make her way from the bed to the bathroom.

A shower did much to restore her spirits. What she had done yesterday might have been foolish, with no thought for consequences, but it had not been criminal. There was no reason for her to have felt quite so shattered. Nevertheless, by the time she emerged from the rondawel into the sunlight, she was feeling slightly apprehensive. The first moments with Roan might be embarrassing.

She need not have worried. The object of her embarrassment was standing talking to Dave. Both men had coffee mugs in their hands, and when they saw her they smiled their good mornings.

'Sleep well, I hope,' Dave commented, and the friendly face held no hint of speculation or leering. 'You're just in time for coffee. There's boiling water in the urn.'

'Thanks.' Gratefully she took a steaming mug from him, then forced herself to look at Roan. The eyes that met hers were friendly, if just a little aloof. And that, she thought with relief, was about as much as she could have hoped for in the circumstances.

A Shengala game warden came to them just then, and while he claimed Dave's attention, Megan said to Roan, 'When will we be going back?'

'Tomorrow morning.'

'I don't believe it!' She stared at him in unconcealed dismay. 'Tomorrow? I thought. . . .'

She stopped, for Dave was already turning back to them. There was just time for Roan to say softly, 'This too shall pass,' and she saw that the aloofness had been chased by a grin.

In the event, it passed pleasantly, and in much the same way as the previous day. There was much that

Roan still wanted to see, to discuss. Megan knew already that he was a man who demanded perfection, not only from those who worked for him, but from himself. She had heard from Ann that each of his holiday resorts lacked nothing in the way of imagination, beauty and amenities. Bronze Mountain would be a jewel in its lovely canyon setting. Evidently his next project would be created with similar care, and as the game park would be the first of its kind for Roan, he was not above learning all he could from someone he evidently respected.

For most of the morning Megan was left to her own devices, but she was far from bored. The camp-grounds reminded her of a small village, not unlike Bronze Mountain in some ways, though perhaps even more self-contained. Overlooking the river, the camp-ground was beautifully situated, and she wondered whether Roan had a similar location in mind for his own game park. As she stood at the fence and looked out over the bush, her eyes searching for game, she wished that just once she could see the park that Roan would make uniquely his own.

Some deer had appeared on the sandy river-bank when Roan came to call her for lunch. 'Sable antelope,' he observed, following the direction of her eyes. 'Look at those horns, Megan, aren't they lovely!' Something in his voice brought a lump to her throat. There was so much more to Roan than superb business acumen. He was a man whose interests covered a broad spectrum, the kind of man who commanded her respect at the same time as he stirred her blood.

As on the previous day, lunch was light and refreshing. It was really too hot in this part of the Lowveld for anything besides fruit and ice-cream at midday. In the late afternoon, when the air was a little cooler, they would go driving again, Dave said, and Megan was pleased. She was eager to see as much as possible.

They were getting into the jeep some hours later when someone called to Dave. The generator had developed a problem, and if Shengala was to have electricity that night it would have to be solved soon.

'Pity.' Dave made a regretful face. 'Seems I'll have to stay here. Look, folks, there's no reason why you shouldn't go.' He held the keys out to Roan. 'Take the jeep rather than your car. It's fantastic for rough terrain.'

Megan wondered if Dave noticed Roan's momentary hesitation. But he took the proffered keys, shrugged, and said, 'Sure, Dave. Thanks.'

It was the second time she had been driven by Roan, Megan thought, as the car made its way slowly along the quiet bushveld road. He drove slowly, but his speed was normal for a game park, where anything more than twenty-five miles per hour was considered a punishable offence. Megan knew already that he was an expert and confident driver. Now, stealing a glance at the rugged profile, she thought he no longer objected to driving with a passenger.

I've achieved something, was her jubilant thought.

Occasionally they stopped. Yesterday Roan had been more interested in water than in game, and that trip had been mainly a matter of business. Today was different.

'You've found out all you wanted to know here at Shengala?' Megan asked.

'More or less.'

This drive through the park was in fact then just a pleasure trip. 'A perk for a stowaway,' Roan grinned, when Megan put the thought into words. 'Keep your eyes skinned, poppet, you don't want to miss anything.'

Poppet—there was a lightness in the word that gave her a moment of intense pleasure. It was so long since she had seen the light side of Roan. The first day she had spent with him, when she had fallen crazily in love with a man whose full name she had not known, seemed a long time ago. The ghost village, and the vlei, could have existed in another world. A world where there had been a Roan and a Megan, where Brendon Stevens and darling Tammy had had no place.

An illusionary world. A magic kind of world. Perhaps that was why it had collapsed with such ease.

Could these last hours together at Shengala have some of that magic? As if the thought alone was self-fulfilling, the drive got off to a delightful start. Not two miles out of camp they came upon a family of monkeys—playful things, swinging on the branches of trees and running along the ground making cheeky gestures at the occupants of the car which had stopped beside them. The birthing season must have been quite recent, as there were four mothers with babies clinging to their bellies.

One monkey, bolder than the rest, jumped on to the car and began to make outrageous gestures. 'Don't open the window,' Roan warned, and Megan shook her head, remembering her mother's long-ago warnings of scalpings.

Frustrated by the two humans who were so heartless as not to give him food, the monkey's gestures became more exaggerated. So comical was the little animal that Megan laughed, and she was unaware that to the man beside her the sound had the ring of music.

'Time to move on,' he said at last.

'With this creature perched on your bonnet?'

'It will jump off soon enough.'

Slowly they went on, and sure enough, half a mile

farther the monkey jumped into the road. Megan was sorry to see it vanish in the tall grass. But there were more animals. Even Roan was surprised at all they saw—giraffe; zebra and wildebeeste, together as usual; and once a herd of buffalo, horns curved, heads lowered at sight of the car.

'They're magnificent!' Megan breathed.

'Lethal too. A bad-tempered buffalo is not an animal to be trifled with.'

If only the ease between them could be permanent. Not for the first time Megan wondered how things would have turned out if she had met Roan when they had not had a linked past.

The afternoon shadows were lengthening on the ground, and Roan had turned the car campwards, when they came upon the herd of impala. Impala were so frequent a sight that after the first herd or two, people rarely stopped to watch them. But this time Roan stopped.

Almost immediately Megan saw that the animals were behaving very strangely. Usually one stag kept watch while the rest of the herd grazed peacefully. But there was nothing peaceful about this herd. They ran without purpose, first one way and then the other. Two impala took the road in front of the car in a graceful yet frantic leap, then leaped back again. There was something hysterical about the animals, a mood that communicated itself to Megan, while she did not understand it.

'What's happening?' she wanted to know.

'Predator,' Roan said briefly.

She caught her breath. 'Can you see it?'

'Not yet.'

'How do the impala know?'

'Smell. Instinct.'

'What do we do?'

'Wait.'

The tension in the herd was growing. Also the feverish purposeless leaping. Megan felt the tension growing within herself. She wanted to leave the scene, and knew they would stay.

'There!' she heard Roan say all at once, his voice low.

She did not know at first what he meant. And then she followed his pointing finger, and her mouth went dry.

A lion was in the bush. It was moving slowly, sleekly, its body all streamlined magnificence, keeping low on the ground. The apprehension within Megan was almost unbearable. Why didn't the impala run away? Why did they remain in the trap?

The lion moved suddenly, and the impala ran. One animal was a little slower than the rest. It was all over in an instant. The lion had the lovely deer pinned down in the long grass.

Megan was rigid. 'That was horrible!' She turned to Roan, her face ashen, her eyes wide with shock. And then her face was against his chest. Her breath came in long shudders, and her fingers clutched convulsively at his shirt.

'Megan.' His arms had gone around her, and he was holding her close. 'Megan, my darling!'

She did not hear the endearment. Her mind was only filled with the horror of what she had seen.

'It was horrible—horrible!' she sobbed against him.

He did not tell her to stop crying. He continued to hold her gently, his hands stroking her hair with a tenderness she perceived rather than thought about.

It was only gradually, when she had stopped crying, that she became aware of Roan as a man, the man she loved. He was all around her. His chest against her cheek, his thighs hard against hers where she lay across his lap. The arms holding her were tender, but there was a contained passion in them all the same.

She tilted back her head to look at him, and was stunned at the hunger in his eyes. As he bent to kiss her, she reached up to meet him. He began to explore the sweetness of her mouth, and she was consumed with a longing that was rapidly becoming familiar.

'God, Megan, I want you so much,' he groaned once, lifting his head.

The blood was pounding in her head, and every nerve in her body tingled with a wild joy. But there was the lion, and if she raised her head she might see the awful thing that had happened.

'Not here,' she whispered.

'We'll go back.'

'Yes.' Her throat was so dry that she could hardly get the word out.

She sat up, and he drew her close beside him, so that their bodies were touching as he drove. They did not speak, no words were necessary. Once he reached out and put an arm around her shoulder and held her tightly, while with the other hand he controlled the wheel.

It came to Megan that he was driving easily. What tension there was in the car was only that of a man and a woman who were longing for a fulfilment which circumstances had denied them too long.

Dave was not about when they drove into camp. 'Why don't you wait for me in the rondawel,' said Roan, his voice urgent as he parked the car. 'I'll just give back these keys.'

It was cool in the thatch-ceilinged room, and just a little dim. Megan stood at the window and waited for Roan to come. There was no shame in her, no fear, no regret. She had waited for Roan since that first day. She loved him, she loved him more than life itself, and what would happen was meant to happen. Fleetingly she thought of Tammy, of her parents—and hoped that if they could see her now they would find it in them to understand and forgive.

She did not have long to wait. She saw him walking across the camp-grounds, long legs brushing the shrubs that bordered the path. She left the window, and when he opened the door she was standing just a few feet away from it.

They looked at each other across the small distance that separated them, dark brown eyes holding green ones, and for a moment they were both quite still. Then Roan let out a groan, 'Megan!' Later she would never remember who moved first. Not that it mattered. The gap between them was closed, and they were holding each other, kissing each other like parched beings whose thirst had to be slaked.

'I want you so much,' he muttered once. 'So much, Megan.'

No mention of love. And even that did not matter. Not any more. She loved enough for them both.

He held her so closely that she thought it was not possible to be closer to another human. 'Made for each other,' he said almost wonderingly. 'We seem to fit together in all the right places.'

The joy in her grew wilder still.

'I want to undress you,' Roan said. 'Will you undress me?'

She had never undressed a man, had not known she could do it. Instinct taught her now. She had not known that the act of undressing and being undressed could be quite so exciting. His shirt was off when she saw the scars that marked his chest. They were no longer raw, but they were vivid enough to be recent. The breath stopped in her throat, and then her fingers traced them lightly. 'The accident?'

'Yes.' The word seemed to be torn from him.

'Oh, Roan—Roan!' Gently, very gently, she touched her lips to one scar, then another, tracing their paths.

As if the action inflamed him, he pulled her to him in a kiss that was so deep and passionate, the sweetness of it so acute, that she gave a stifled moan of pleasure. His hands began to move over her, shaping the curves of her body between his fingers, moulding them in his hands.

'Why do you have to be so beautiful?' he asked raggedly.

'You think I'm beautiful?' she asked wonderingly, joyfully.

'The most beautiful woman in the world.'

He picked her up and carried her to the bed—as he had done last night. But that was where the similarity ended. This time there would be no drawing back. It did not matter that Roan did not love her, that all he felt for her was physical desire. It did not matter that there could be no future for them. She loved him. She wanted to be with him as a woman is with a man she truly loves. That was the only reality, the only meaning.

He was breathing fast as he put her down on the bed, and she knew that he wanted her as much as she wanted him. He lay down beside her and gathered her to him, his hands caressing her bare body, his lips kissing her. And she was kissing him too, while her hands explored his shoulders, his back, his hips. While she learned the shape of this man who was dearer to her than she had ever thought a person could be.

His mouth began an erotic exploration of her throat before moving to her breasts, kissing first the one then the other. She was ecstatic beneath his touch. She had never experienced a joy and a sexual freedom like this, and she tightened her arms around his back.

When he pulled away from her—abruptly—she could only look at him dazed.

'Roan?'

'It's no good.'

'It is! You know it is!'

'No, Megan.' He was breathing raggedly. 'I can't go on.'

She felt dazed, numb. 'I don't understand. . . .'

'I know you don't.'

He got up from the bed and went to the window. She lay where she was for a moment, and all she could think was, 'He's rejected me. He doesn't want me.'

And then the blur that was in her eyes cleared, and she saw Roan's back. The muscles were bunched in his shoulders and at the back of his neck. He was six feet two inches of rigidity. And her heart went out to him.

Quickly she left the bed too, and went to him. She did not know if he heard the soft footfalls of her bare feet, because he did not turn. She came up close behind him and touched him, and felt him flinch as her fingers made contact with the tight muscles in his shoulders.

'Megan, don't!' The words were torn from him.

'Why not?'

'I don't want it.'

'You wanted it a few minutes ago.' Was this Megan pleading? Asking a man to make love to her? Megan, who had never even slept with a man?

'Yes!' He turned then, and she gasped at the torment in his eyes. 'I started this, but I shouldn't have.'

'Why, Roan, why?'

He passed a hand in front of his eyes. 'I can't talk about it. Don't press me, Megan.'

'Roan. . . .'

'Get dressed. I'll dress too.' His voice was flat.

'Just like that.'

In a low voice he said, 'I'm sorry. Please believe me.'

They did not talk as they dressed. The silence in the rondawel was oppressive, not the silence of friends—or lovers—it was the silence of two people who were too acutely aware of each other, and embarrassed by the awareness.

Roan left the rondawel first. It was almost dark by the time Megan went outside. She did not feel like eating, but she knew that a semblance of normalcy was important, and she walked over to Dave's rondawel, where a fire had already been lit. Dave asked about the drive, and Roan told him what they had seen. Looking at him, Megan saw that the look of torment had gone, but she noticed that he did not tell Dave about the lion's kill.

They sat at the fire a long time that night. Each time the embers died Dave put on new logs, and Megan was glad, wanting to postpone for as long as possible the moment when she and Roan would have to go back to the rondawel together.

In the event, she went first, Roan making an excuse to have a last word with Dave. Megan recognised the excuse for what it was, and by the time Roan opened the door she was in bed. As she listened to him pushing the chairs together she kept her breathing slow and steady, just as if she was asleep, but she doubted that he was fooled.

They left Shengala early the next morning, and the only words that passed between them were when they were still with Dave. An act put on for Dave's benefit. As Roan drove slowly through the wakening bushveld, Megan kept her eyes on the bush beyond her window, not because she was interested in seeing game—a leopard could have crossed the road in front of her today and she doubted if she would be excited—but because it gave her an excuse not to look at Roan. They were near the park gates when they came upon a family of cavorting baboons, but Roan did not stop. It was as if he knew that there was no point in it.

Leaving Shengala, they came to the road that would take them back to Bronze Mountain. The car gathered speed. The slow twenty-five mile per hour speed limit that was essential for the roads of a game park was inappropriate on a highway. Involuntarily Megan turned her head, and was immediately sorry.

The tension was back. The hands that held the wheel were tight-knuckled, the rugged profile of the driver was taut. On the morning when Megan had concealed herself beneath the tarpaulin she had been so sure that she was doing the right thing. Now she knew she had solved nothing. If anything, the problem was perhaps even worse than before.

CHAPTER NINE

The mural covered much of the wall. Soon it would be finished, and then Megan would have to leave Bronze Mountain. There was no sense of satisfaction as she stood back and looked at her work. It was taking place steadily. It was good; everyone who came into the recreation hall had nothing but praise for it. Yet the further the work progressed, the more desperate Megan became.

She was reminded of the legend of the *Odyssey*, of the faithful Penelope. When Odysseus had set sail for the Trojan War, leaving his wife behind him, there had come a time when it seemed that he would never return. There were many many suitors who wanted to marry Penelope, and eventually, under duress, she had given her promise to marry when the garment she was weaving was finished. But Penelope had not wanted to marry anyone else, and so every night she undid some of the work she had done that day.

Megan felt a little like Penelope. If only she could paint over some of the mural! If there was a way of halting the work, delaying it—a way to stay longer at Bronze Mountain. Roan would never love her, she knew that, but she could not leave Bronze Mountain while his problem was unresolved. She would *not*.

She did not know when the idea came to her. An idea that startled her at first as much as the thought of stowing away had done. Could she do it? She had to! For she knew by now that she was the only one who could give Roan back his confidence in himself.

The situation she would find herself in would not be unfamiliar. But previously there had been a detail she had omitted.

There was a party on the night she decided to put her plan into operation. There was a braaivleis, and when everyone had eaten someone brought out a tape-deck and people danced. The atmosphere was lighthearted. Only Megan was tense. Roan made no move to approach her. It was Larry who tried to monopolise her, who tried to dance holding her close. Towards the end of the evening he wanted her to walk with him, away from the dancing into the shadows. Only a walk, he said, when she refused, but Megan knew there was more on his mind, and she could not bear the thought of being in his arms. There was only one man she wanted to be with in that way.

Besides, it was time for her plan. Gently but firmly she told Larry she was tired, then slipped away from the scene.

Roan was whistling when he opened the door of his cabin. He switched on the light and threw his jacket on to a chair. And then his eyes fell on his bed, and the whistling died on his lips.

'Megan!'

It was almost impossible to smile when her heart was beating so violently that it threatened to burst through her chest.

'Hello, Roan.'

'What the hell are you doing here?'

Some women might be to the role of the seductress born; Megan was not. Though she had rehearsed the scene in her mind, now she could only wet her lips nervously. 'Isn't it obvious?'

'Get out!'

She got off the bed and came to him. 'Roan.'

He took a step backwards. 'Don't let's start this again.'

'Please kiss me.'

A muscle moved in his throat. 'You're playing a dangerous game,' he said roughly.

'Kiss me.' She came closer to him, and she saw the sweat standing out on his face.

'Why don't you go, Megan?'

'You know why.' She could feel herself starting to tremble.

'And you know that we've been through all this before.' His breathing was a little ragged. 'Do you think we could stop after a kiss?'

'I don't want to stop.'

He pulled her into his arms, and kissed her hungrily. She clung to him, feeling the hard length of his body against her, knowing that he wanted her as much as she wanted him.

It would work! This time it would work!

And then he thrust her from him.

'Roan. . . .'

'You're a single-minded woman, Megan, I've told you that before. Don't you ever give up?'

'I will when you stop fighting me.'

'We've been over this, dammit! We could have made love at Shengala, but I. . . .' He paused. Then he said, 'Nothing's changed.'

'It has.' She took a breath. 'I love you.'

Tell me that you love me too. At least say something—anything. I can't stand this silence, and that look on your face.

At last he said, flatly, 'I'm flattered.'

Megan flinched. 'That's all?'

'What more is there?'

I was crazy to come here, she thought. I can take just so much, I don't think I can take any more.

From somewhere she dredged up a strength she had not known she possessed. 'You say I'm single-minded. You are too, Roan. You won't let me help you. You need me, I know you do.'

'That's enough!' He barked out the words.

'I love you and you need me.'

'All I need is for you to get out of this cabin.' His face was a mask, cold and impenetrable. 'Go, please, Megan. Now.'

She went then. Blindly, numbly, she went. Out into the darkness where the crickets shrilled and the baboons barked from the distant mountain reaches. Knowing she had done what she could, that she could do no more.

Knowing too that Roan was finally lost to her.

When a figure stepped into her path she let out a cry. 'Megan!' A man's voice. For a moment she thought it was Roan, that he'd decided to come after her, to make up.

'Megan,' said the person again, and it wasn't Roan at all, it was Larry.

'Larry,' she said weakly. 'You gave me a fright!'

'So I see.'

'You're going for a walk?'

'I was looking for you.'

'Oh. . . .'

'Oh,' he mocked. 'You'd vanished from the party. I went to your cabin, and you weren't there either. And then I saw you coming out of Roan's cabin.'

Her head came up. 'Why does this sound like an accusation?'

'What were you doing there? With that man?'

Until now she had always liked Larry. Not in the

blood-stirring way that was reserved for Roan, but affectionately. It came to her now that she did not like him very much at all.

'I don't think I owe you any explanations,' she said very quietly. 'Goodnight, Larry.'

'Oh no, you don't,' he ground out, as she made to go past him. 'What is Roan to you, Megan?'

'I told you, I don't owe you any explanations.'

Again she tried to walk past him, but he seized her and pulled her to him. 'He's not for you, just as he wasn't for Tammy.'

'Let me go!' She squirmed in hands that held her fast.

'Tammy at least had some sense—even though she was killed for it in the end.'

Megan stopped her struggling. 'Roan didn't kill Tammy,' she said at last.

'Not deliberately,' Larry acknowledged.

'It was an accident, you know that. It could have happened to anyone.'

'It needn't have happened. Shouldn't have.'

The blood was ice in her veins. 'What are you trying to say?'

'Only that the high-and-mighty Brendon Stevens has to have every woman in sight.'

'That's not true!'

'He can't stand to see a woman prefer another man. Haven't you cottoned on to that yet? My God, Megan, I ask you to dance and you freeze in my arms, then you go running off to sleep with Roan!'

'I didn't sleep with him, as it happens. Tell me about Tammy.'

'Roan fancied her,' said Larry. 'She preferred me.'

'You're leaving something out.'

It was very dark, there was not enough moonlight to see Larry's face by. Tilting her head back, Megan strained her eyes, wishing she could see his expression. This moment was important, instinct told her that.

At last he said, 'There was a party. Tammy was with Roan, but then she realised she wanted to be with me.'

'Go on!' Megan urged, when he paused. He *had* to go on, though with every fibre of her being she knew that this was one story she would hate to hear.

'Roan was jealous. He walked out, forced Tammy to go with him. He must have been in a devil of a temper when he set out for Bronze Mountain—probably raced like a madman. The rest you know.'

The accident. The loss of Tammy's life. She knew it all.

But perhaps there were things she did not know after all. Logic told Megan that Larry had to be speaking at least part of the truth. There had never been any doubt that Roan had been the driver of the car. And there had to be a reason for Roan's lack of confidence in his driving.

Yet instinct, a special instinct linking her to Roan whom she loved, even now, told her that there was more to the story. That there were facts she had to hear, even if she had to force them from Larry.

'There's more,' she said.

He hesitated. 'No.'

'Yes!'

'It's late.' The hands dropped from her shoulders, and now it was Megan who detained him, seizing his wrist when he made to walk on.

'We have to talk,' she said.

'It's late.'

'Not that late. There's something you're hiding from me.'

'Don't be silly.'

'I want to know what happened that night,' she insisted.

'You know it already.' Perhaps it was the darkness of the night that made her extra-sensitive to his voice. Like a blind person, she thought, substituting sound for sight. Larry was on the defensive, and she had to know why.

'What happened at that party, Larry?' She spoke with a firmness and an authority she had not known she possessed. 'I want to know everything.'

Something of her tone must have got through to him, for she felt the stiffening in the wrist beneath her fingers, the rigidity of the muscles in the body so close to hers. Larry was tense, but the tension had a different cause from that which Roan experienced; moment by moment Megan understood that more clearly.

'All right then,' he conceded finally, in a tone heavy with resentment, 'I'll tell you. Tammy came with Roan. She'd been out with him once or twice—God knows what the attraction is that devil has with women.'

'You're side tracking.' Megan stifled a feeling of quite unjustified jealousy. Tammy had been so lovely, it was no wonder Roan had liked her.

'I asked her to dance, cut in on them. Don't suppose Roan liked that, not that he could do anything about it. He may be the big boss here at Bronze Mountain, but that's as far as it goes.'

'Go on, Larry!' Megan's fingers dug into the hard-boned wrist.

'Tammy enjoyed dancing with me, we had fun together. Afterwards. . . .' He paused.

'Afterwards?' Megan prompted, aware of a heightening tension.

'She . . . she came with me to the bar.'

'You drank together?'

'We had a couple of drinks. You're not going to make anything of that!'

'You were drunk?'

'Happy. Not drunk, just a little happy.'

Drunk, Megan thought sickened, without giving voice to the thought. She said only, 'Roan objected?'

'As you might imagine. Dour fellow that he is, he couldn't stand to see others enjoying themselves. Specially not the girl he came with. I suppose it offended that ridiculous sense of dignity.'

Roan's dignity had not been offended. Roan was so much a man that he had no need to stand on his dignity. It was his sense of responsibility that had come into play. Megan saw the scene as clearly as if she had been there. Tammy, frivolous after a little too much to drink, flirting with Larry who would have been more her type than Roan could ever have been—Larry was right about that. Larry, drunk, hostile at the fact that Roan was insisting on going back to Bronze Mountain with the girl he had brought to the party. And Roan, cold and angry and very much in command of himself and of those around him.

'There was a fight?' Roan would have won it had there been one.

'No fight. Roan just kind of force-marched Tammy out of the place. It was the last time I saw her alive.'

Larry's voice broke a little at the last words, and looking up at him in the darkness, Megan felt a moment of sympathy with him. Shallow he might be, but perhaps Larry had genuinely liked her sister, had been even more affected by her death than she had realised up till now.

'So now you know everything.' The sullenness was back.

'Yes,' Megan said gently. 'Thank you.'

Larry walked back with her to her cabin and said goodnight. Megan watched him vanish in the darkness. She did not open the door after that, instead she walked away from the cabin, taking the path that led towards the edge of the canyon. It was the path she had taken the first night, after she had found out that Roan was Brendon Stevens. Since then she had come to know it well. She was a person who did her best thinking out of doors, and the trail to the canyon had become her favourite.

There was a viewing point at the end of the trail. There were some rocks there, and also a bench, so that those who wanted to sit and look into the purple reaches of the mountains could relax. Megan chose the rocks. All day the sun had burned down on them, and though the air was cool, the smooth stone still held some warmth. She leaned back, letting her body curve with the shape of the stone, bending her knees and resting her chin on her hands.

In the past weeks she had come to know this view of the canyon well, yet she never tired of it. Each time she saw it, it looked different. There was the mood of dawn, when the bushes on the cliff edge were webbed with dew, and the mountains looked brooding and forbidding. When the sun came up, there was the lushness of forests, the vivid colours of the wild flowers that grew in the long rough grass, and the ruggedness of the mountains, each with its own shape and unique character. Later would come sunset, and the mountains would be fired with the light of a dying sun. Bronze Mountain, higher than the others, and with its upper reaches completely devoid of vegetation, would be gilded with the startling bronze shade that had given it its name. Megan guessed that more photos would be taken of Bronze Mountain than of any other view in the area.

Now, in the darkness, there was yet another mood. The night was clear and cloudless, and the sky was filled with a myriad stars. The stars ended where the mountains began, black and sharply edged against the vivid sky. The first time Megan had come here at night, the mountains had been great dark humps, formless somehow, and mysterious. Now that she knew them better, she could identify each individual shape.

Megan, who had lived all her life in a tidy city suburb, had come to love the mountains and the bushveld, the sweet-smelling air and the stillness. As she looked up at Bronze Mountain, a more imposing silhouette than the others, she knew that she would miss this place when she left it.

Most of all she would miss Roan. The missing would be as acute as any physical pain. And it would begin soon. When she left Bronze Mountain.

'Now you know everything,' Larry had said. It was true that she knew far more than before. Enough to hazard some guesses. Enough to know that they had all been wrong about Roan. All? Ann had believed in him. There had been a conversation with her cabin-mate which came back to Megan now, a conversation when Ann had implied that the truth about the fatal night had never been disclosed. But even Ann did not know the facts. Only Roan knew those.

At last Megan knew what to do. She would choose her time carefully. Twice she had acted on impulse, and both times her plans had misfired. The third time had to be handled correctly.

It was one thing to know what to do, harder to pin Roan down. It was as if after the scene in his room he was determined to avoid her. It was a Saturday afternoon when Megan met him just as he was coming out of the store and she stopped him. 'Hello, Roan.'

'Hello, Megan.' The words were said in mid-step, just as if she was an acquaintance with whom he was only on formal greeting terms. He was going to walk on, and she put her hand on his arm to detain him. 'I'd like to talk to you.'

'Oh?' Dark eyes narrowed. And then he said, 'Well?'

I'm *not* a stranger, she wanted to say, and I've done nothing to deserve this kind of treatment. But she kept the words in check. 'In private.'

'We're private now.'

'Where we won't be interrupted.' She looked up at him, loving him, yet wishing that it was easier to get through to him. 'May I come to your cabin?'

'I don't think that's such a good idea,' he remarked drily.

The implication was not lost on her, and she flushed. 'It's important. Roan, please!'

His expression as he looked down at her was hard to read. For a long moment she wondered if he meant to refuse her. Then something moved suddenly in his face. 'All right.'

She drew a breath of relief. 'Now?'

The gaze that rested on her mouth was enigmatic. 'Later.' He glanced at his watch. 'In about two hours, shall we say?'

Two hours. Long enough to rehearse again what she wanted to say to him. To tell him what she had found out from Larry, to ask Roan to tell her the rest. To let him know that she was able to imagine much of what had happened on the night of the accident, that he should stop protecting Tammy and that he should give her, Megan, the actual details.

Two hours had never passed so slowly. A hundred

times she glanced at her watch. Ann's eyes were on her, curious and amused. 'What are you up to this time?' she asked, but Megan smiled and shook her head. After the weeks of sharing a cabin Ann had become a dear friend, more especially she was the one person who would understand what Megan was going to do. But Megan had reached a stage where to talk about Roan was to invade a personal sense of privacy that went too deep for sharing.

She was a little nervous as she approached his cabin, for she knew that this attempt had to succeed—there could be no others. She knocked on the door, and as it opened she said eagerly, 'Roan. . . .' then stopped. For it was not Roan who stood facing her; it was Petra. Petra, wearing only a transparent slip, with apparently nothing underneath.

'Why, Megan!' If the other girl was discomfited there was nothing to show it. 'Were you looking for Roan?'

Megan felt suddenly ill as the colour drained from her face, and her legs went weak. 'It doesn't matter,' she said unsteadily.

'I'll call him.'

'No!'

She was about to turn away when she heard Petra call, 'Roan! Roan darling, come out here.'

'No!' Megan jerked out, and wheeled.

Not fast enough. She was still in the doorway when the familiar voice said, 'Megan,' and she stood still.

'Megan,' he said again, and she turned, very slowly.

He was smiling at her, though in her fevered state she did not notice that the smile was strained. She saw only the rumpled hair, the bare feet and bare chest. All he wore was a pair of shorts.

'I remember now.' His voice was light. 'We'd arranged to meet. Aren't you a little early?'

'No.' Megan cursed herself for an unsteadiness which she could not control.

'I didn't realise the time had gone so quickly.' He glanced at Petra. 'Megan wanted a word with me, do you mind?'

Before the other girl could answer, Megan's pride came to her rescue. 'It's really not important,' she said, lifting her head. 'I'll be on my way.'

'Sure?' Roan asked.

'Of course.'

Tears were gathering and she was determined that neither Roan nor Petra would have the satisfaction of seeing them. Quickly, before Roan could say anything to stop her, she spun away.

Later she would not remember the headlong dash along the path, away from the cabins, from the resort. She would remember only the need to get away from Bronze Mountain, from eyes that might be either curious or sympathetic. The desperate need to be alone.

She took the first path she came across, not knowing where it led, not caring. Across a gully, over a natural rock bridge, and then a little later along the bank of a stream. She had never been this way, and she saw none of it.

When she came into a wooded area she was glad. It was dark here, with the trees shutting out the sun. A place where she could be quite alone in her unhappiness and despair.

Despair was a tangible thing, filling her chest, gnawing at her insides. Megan had known unhappiness before now; like any normal person she had experienced times of sadness. There had been the terrible grief when Tammy had died. But the emotion she felt now was something different. It was numbing, chilling, she did not know how to cope with it.

The first two efforts to reach Roan had been unsuccessful. There was no reason, really, why this last one should have been any different, but she had been so certain it would be. What she had not anticipated, could *not* have anticipated, was the terrible humiliation he had meted out to her. In those first moments when she had run from the cabin, wanting only to be alone, she had been in a state of shock. Loving Roan as she did, seeing Petra in his cabin, had been a terrible shock. It was a sight which would remain with her a long time. She would make every effort to forget it, but she knew that though she might eventually be able to banish it from her waking thoughts, it would remain to haunt her dreams at night. She could see Roan and Petra making love just as surely as if she'd been in the room with them at the time.

In those first moments there had been only the shock, the mindless running away. When she was out of sight of Bronze Mountain there were the blessed tears that ran down her cheeks unchecked. Now, in the cool dimness of the forest, the nature of her emotion was beginning to change. Blind facts began to assume meaning.

It was no coincidence that Petra had opened the door to her. Roan had known that Petra was coming, and that they would make love, just as he had known that Megan was coming to talk to him. It was Roan who had suggested a time for their meeting. He had known full well that when Megan came to the cabin the other girl would be with him.

Why? Why, why, why? The word echoed in her mind. Thundered.... Couldn't Roan simply have told her that he was in love with Petra? Hard as it would have been, Megan would have found a way of accepting it. Yet knowing full well that she loved him—she had told him so just two days earlier—Roan had set out to humiliate her. A brutal humiliation.

Why?

The path became difficult to follow, and she was forced to walk more slowly. Had Megan been less preoccupied, she would have noticed the change in scenery, would have been fascinated by the fact that the pine forests cultivated by man had given way to untamed jungle. There were no tidy rows of trees now, there was just a mass of wild undergrowth. Trees with roots sprawling on top of the ground, with stems growing tall and thin in the constant struggle to reach the light. Moss everywhere, clinging to rocks and fallen logs, and toadstools of every size and colour. Overhead a canopy of foliage, so dense that almost no light could penetrate.

Further she went, and further, while painful thoughts whirled in her head. It was the chill air which eventually took her out of her preoccupation. For the first time she realised that it was getting dark. Time to be turning back.

Looking around her for the first time, she turned to go back the way she had come. Once she stumbled on a mass of roots, but she thrust out a hand and caught herself on a tree-trunk before she reached the ground. A little farther on she saw a waterfall cascading down a pile of rock, and she looked at it thoughtfully, wondering how she could have missed it earlier. But she did not stop, because it was getting darker, and she knew she had to get back to Bronze Mountain before nightfall.

On she went, walking as fast as she could, wishing that the trail was more distinct. Fear was beginning to stir in her, for it was getting darker and darker, and she saw nothing she recognised. At least she was on a trail, a discarded cigarette carton in the moss told her that. No matter that the carton was soggy and old, it was good to know that hikers had once been this way.

At a jumble of roots and moss she stopped. The path, such as it had been, had petered out. She had no idea which way to go. She was lost. Finally she had to acknowledge it to herself.

Roan! She wasn't sure if she had actually called him, or whether it was just that his name pounded so hard in her mind that she could hear it. Roan, find me! I'm lost!

But Roan would not find her. Roan was with Petra. He did not know that Megan was in a jungle that was so far off the beaten track that only an occasional enterprising hiker came this way. He did not know she was lost.

Nobody knew.

Ann. . . . Ann would worry. But when? Later tonight, perhaps, when Megan failed to come to the cabin. Not before then.

What could she do? A screech rent the silent air, and Megan clapped a hand over her mouth to stifle a scream. A moment later she saw a flurry of wings as a brightly-plumaged bird thrust upwards through the foliage of a near-by tree.

Shuddering, she glanced wildly about her. She could not stay here. She had to get out, quickly, before night descended over this horrible place. She had to!

And that was impossible. The shuddering increased as she accepted the fact. She would not get out of the jungle tonight.

It was cold—very cold—and getting steadily darker. She could die here, she knew that quite suddenly. The thought was accompanied by a sudden wave of hysteria. She thought of the impala, and how hysterical they had been when the lion was near by. It was a hysteria which she quelled in minutes. Unless she did something about it, she really would die of exposure. She had to think, and to do that she had to be calm.

It was an icy calm that descended on her as she tried to remember what she knew of survival techniques. Protection from the cold, that was important, doubly so because she did not even have a sweater with her. 'Why do I never have a sweater at the crises of my life?' she asked herself with a momentary flash of humour. And animals—there could be animals in the jungle. How best to protect herself from them? She had no sweater, no food. She did not even have matches to light a fire. All around her was nothing but moss and leaves.

Leaves! Suddenly she knew what she had to do. She began to sweep the leaves together with her hands, until a huge pile of them lay on the ground. Here and there were some pebbles, and she put a few in the pocket of her jeans. She would get thirsty, and she recalled reading somewhere that sucking a pebble could allay thirst for a while. Complete darkness was almost upon her when she buried herself beneath the pile of leaves. She could only hope that they would serve the double purpose of isolating her from the cold, and keeping her scent from reaching marauding animals.

The night was darker than any Megan had experienced at Bronze Mountain, where the sky had been alive with stars. In the jungle the dense canopy of tangled foliage shut out both starlight and moonlight. It was a long night. Now and then she dozed briefly, but soon she would wake. Beneath the dank-smelling cover of leaves she waited for the dawn.

While survival had been uppermost in her mind she had not thought of Roan, but in the long hours beneath the leaves he was almost constantly on her mind. Her thoughts were not pleasant ones. There had been memories that she had intended to cherish, but now she could only think of Roan as she had seen him last—almost naked, with Petra beside him. Once more she could see them making love together. It was a picture that gave her such anguish that she tried to push it from her, but it returned again and again.

She must have dozed once more shortly before dawn. When she woke up the forest was bathed in a kind of translucent greyness, it was just light enough to make out the shapes of the trees closest to her. She had woken suddenly, and as she lay stiffly beneath the leaves she thought she heard voices. I'm hallucinating, she told herself, I have to get a grip on myself.

The voices grew louder, and there was the sound of barking. She was not hallucinating! Struggling to sit up, she shouted, 'Help! Help!'

She was still beneath the leaves when they reached her. A dog burst through the trees first, behind him a man.

'Roan?' The strangled cry came through parched lips.

'Megan! Oh, Megan!' In an instant he was beside her, pushing away some of the leaves, cradling her in his arms. 'Megan, my darling, are you hurt?'

CHAPTER TEN

IN those first moments she was so relieved to be rescued that she forgot to be angry with him. There was just the joy of being close to him.

'Are you hurt?' he asked again, his voice ragged. Megan wanted to answer him, but after the hours without water her mouth was so dry that talking was difficult. She could only shake her head.

'Thank God we found you!' His arms had tightened around her, and she felt his lips in her hair.

Two more men appeared in the half-light, stopping in their tracks at the sight of Roan and Megan on the ground, an excited dog beside them. 'You found her!' exclaimed one of the men, and Megan recognised Anton, the engineer who had driven her back from the dam-site.

'Huddled under these leaves.' Roan sounded as strange as Megan had ever heard him. 'She must have spent the whole night here.'

'Can she walk back, or shall we get help?'

'I'll carry her,' said Roan.

'I can walk,' Megan's voice was a whisper over the dryness.

'A stretcher,' said Brian, the second of the two men. 'We'll go back for the stretcher.'

'I'll carry her,' Roan said savagely.

'It's a long way,' Brian protested.

'I'll carry her. Where's the water canteen?'

Roan brushed more of the leaves from Megan's body, then he brought her up to rest against his arm while with his free hand he held the canteen to her mouth. All his movements were gentle. To Megan the water was the finest liquid she had ever tasted, but Roan did not let her have much of it. She would be sick if she did, he said, soon he would give her more.

The canteen was re-corked and given back to Anton, then Roan was lifting Megan into his arms. It was a long walk back. Now and then they stopped to rest a few minutes. Anton and Brian offered to take turns carrying Megan, but Roan refused. Megan did not know whether to be glad or not. She was acutely aware of the hard chest and arms all around her, and she had to will her senses not to respond. Loving Roan had brought her no joy.

They came at last to Bronze Mountain and Ann opened the door of the cabin before the men had a chance to knock. 'You found her!' she exclaimed. 'Oh, thank God! Megan, what happened?'

'She'll talk later.' Roan sounded savage again, and as strange as before. 'She must get to bed.'

Megan slept most of the day. Now and then she woke, and twice she saw that Roan was sitting by her bed, but they did not talk. When she finally sat up it was evening and Ann was in the room.

'I'm starving!' Megan declared.

'Soup and some toast,' said Ann.

'I could eat an ox, I'm so hungry.'

'Start with something light.' Ann came to the bed and hugged her. 'Heavens, but you had us worried! I thought Roan would go out of his mind!'

Megan stared at her, forgetting her hunger. 'When he brought me back, do you mean?'

'No, idiot, during the night, when I realised you were missing.'

'You went to Roan?'

'Wasn't he the obvious person to go to?' Ann asked gently. 'Think about it, Megan, and stop looking so stricken. I'm going to get you that soup.'

Food had never tasted so good. Presently Megan pushed the tray to one side and looked at Ann. 'Why was Roan obvious?' she asked.

'Because there's been something between the two of you from the beginning. You're in love with him.'

'No!' She dropped her eyes and shifted restlessly beneath the sheets. After a moment she looked up. 'All right then, perhaps I am. I don't fool you, I know that. But Roan's in love with Petra.'

'Nonsense,' Ann said succinctly.

Megan could not tell her friend about the scene in Roan's cabin. There were some things that could not be put into words. Besides, the situation was one she had not yet come to terms with herself. Perhaps she never would. 'I happen to know that he loves her,' was all she said.

'And I happen to know that he sat by your bed hour after hour, just watching you. I've seen the expression on his face, Megan. Not the expression of a man in love with another woman.'

Guilt, Megan thought. He feels guilty because he knows how I felt when I came to his cabin. He knows that he humiliated me.

She changed the subject. 'What happened last night?'

'I found you missing. How did you get into the jungle, Megan? What on earth possessed you to go that way?'

'I . . . I went for a walk. . . . I suppose I didn't realise how far I'd gone. I'm so sorry.'

'So you should be,' Ann said feelingly. 'Roan wasn't the only one in a state. I wanted to search too, but I had to wait here in case you were found, and I thought I'd go crazy.'

'I'm so sorry—so terribly sorry. Tell me what happened.'

'I got back to the cabin late last night, and you weren't here. At first I thought you'd gone out for dinner and were late coming back, but eventually I started to worry.'

'You went to Roan?'

'Right. I've never seen a man quite so distraught.'

Megan knew she shouldn't ask the question, but she asked it all the same. 'Was Petra with him?'

'Of course not. We scoured the grounds, and there was no sign of you. Then Roan organised search parties.'

'I feel terrible,' sighed Megan, thinking of all the trouble and worry she had caused. 'What made Roan think of looking in the jungle?'

'Larry saw you walking towards the pine forest in the late afternoon.'

'Larry?' Megan stared incredulously. 'I didn't see him.' But then in the state of mind she had been in at the time she could have walked through a crowd of people without noticing them.

'Unfortunately he didn't think of stopping you. Roan had search parties in the forest, but it was dark and they could see nothing. Very early this morning they set out again, with a tracker dog this time and one of your shoes.'

Megan leaned back against the pillow. 'So that's how he found me!'

'You look tired,' her friend told her. 'Why don't you get some more sleep? Roan's coming by in the morning.'

Megan felt a thrill of alarm. 'I don't want to see him.'

'He wants to see you.'

'Tell him I've left the country.'

'I don't think Roan wants to send a tracker dog after you twice in two days!' Ann laughed. 'Get some rest, I have a feeling you may need it!'

Roan came to the cabin the next morning. Megan knew exactly what he would say—so much so that she had rehearsed her own responses during the night.

Oddly, he did not launch straight away into a furious criticism of her impulsiveness. He stood in the doorway, looking at her across the room. In his eyes there was none of the coldness which Megan had come to expect from him lately. Instead there was an expression which made her pulses race. In the circumstances it was hard to maintain a coolness of her own.

Moments passed, and then she said a little too quickly, 'Thanks for rescuing me.'

'Don't thank me.'

'But, Roan. . . .'

'We'll talk later,' he told her softly.

The scene was not proceeding at all as she had visualised it. 'Later?' she asked uncertainly.

'I want to take you somewhere. Will you come with me, Megan?'

Of course I won't. After the way you've behaved I wouldn't do anything with you, go anywhere with you.

'I don't think so.'

'Please,' said Roan.

Please? The word sounded strange coming from his lips.

'There's no point. After what happened. . . .' Megan stopped, catching her upper lip between her teeth.

Something moved in his throat. 'You've every right to refuse, but it would mean a lot to me if you came.'

An order she would have defied. This strange gentle plea was harder to resist.

'All right,' she agreed after a moment.

As they left the cabin, she asked, 'Where are we going?'

The tall man smiled down at her. 'You'll see.'

They would walk or go on horseback, she thought, and was astonished when Roan led her to the resort car instead. She looked up at him. 'We're driving?'

'Yes.' His hand was on the door, opening it for her.

'Why, Roan?' she asked, when the car had left Bronze Mountain.

He took his eyes from the road and met hers. 'Because it's time.'

A lump came suddenly to her throat and she turned her eyes to the window so that he would not see her emotion. It was amazing that after the way he had behaved he still had the power to move her so deeply. I didn't know love could be like this, Megan thought, as she stared unseeingly over a vista of pine forests. I thought love would be fun and uncomplicated and beautiful. I didn't know it could hurt, that it could defy all reason.

'Enjoying the scenery?' she heard him ask.

'It's beautiful,' she answered, and wondered if he knew that it meant nothing to her.

Where were they going? For the first time she let her eyes focus on the countryside beyond the window. The road was not one that she recognised. What was Roan up to?

They left the highway after a while and took a narrow sand road, slowing at a clump of willows. Megan gasped with sudden recognition. Spinning round, she looked at Roan, and found him waiting for her. 'The vlei!'

His eyes were deep with an expression that made her heart race. 'Yes, Megan, the vlei.'

A little bumpily she said, 'I didn't recognise this road.'

'That's because you've never been on it before. The other times you came on horseback, along veld trails, remember?'

There's nothing about those other times that I've forgotten. Sometimes I wish that I *could* forget. 'I remember,' she said aloud, trying to keep her voice casual.

She watched him turn off the ignition and get out of the car. She herself remained where she was, her whole body seized by sudden trembling. Roan walked around the car and opened her door, and he held out his hand to her. 'Come, Megan.'

Somehow she managed to control at least the outward manifestations of the trembling as she took his hand and got out of the car. She dropped his hand as soon as her feet had touched the ground and he made no comment.

They walked together over the scrub towards the path. The path was narrow, so that they had to walk close together, but they did not speak. Megan had nothing to say, and she knew already that Roan was not one for small talk.

In the clearing they stopped. The scene that met their eyes was idyllic. The sun was shining, shafting through the willows on to the soft wild grass; shining on the vlei, giving the water the appearance of spun glass. Between the reeds swam the ducks. They had changed in the time since Megan and Roan had seen them last. They had grown in size, and they were covered with feathers. Six funny lively balls of gold.

Megan and Roan stood at the water's edge a few

minutes, watching them. At last Megan said, 'They're adorable.'

'They are,' Roan agreed lightly.

He's not really interested in the ducks, came the thought. His mind isn't on them. Mine isn't either.

Still with her eyes on the water, she said, 'Did you bring me here to see the ducks?'

'No.'

The trembling started again. 'Then why?'

'To talk.' He was staring out over the water just as she was, but she felt his arm brush hers, and the skin where they touched was alive with sudden electricity.

He had said earlier that they would talk. She looked up at him. 'Why here, Roan? Because it's private?'

He looked down at her then, and there was an expression in his eyes which reminded her of the first time they had been here. She held her breath. 'Because,' said Roan, 'this is where we fell in love. We did fall in love, didn't we, when I was just Roan and you were just Megan?'

Joy was a wild thing inside her. Her heart was in her eyes as she looked at him. And then she remembered all that had happened since then, all that had happened yesterday. 'That was a long time ago,' she said jerkily.

'A few days ago you told me you loved me.' His voice was very low. 'Have you changed your mind?'

'No.' She had spoken the truth without thinking. On a harder note she said, 'Don't play games with me.'

'*I* haven't changed my mind.' It was as if he hadn't heard her.

'I don't understand. . . . '

'This was where we fell in love. I know I fell in love with you here, Megan.'

'You really mean you . . .?' She paused, and as reality

returned she turned to him. 'Things have changed since then.'

He had turned to her too. A hand reached out to cup her chin. She wanted to look away from him, and had no option but to meet his eyes.

'You know they've changed,' she insisted. 'There's Petra.'

'Ah, Petra.' Roan looked suddenly grim.

'You love her now.'

'Petra doesn't mean a thing to me,' he said crisply.

'You were making love to her.'

He dropped his hand. 'Petra and I have never made love.'

'But the two of you . . . in your cabin. . . .'

'An act—for your benefit.' Roan's expression was sombre. 'And my God, look what happened! You did run off because of what you saw, Megan?'

'Yes,' she admitted after a moment. 'Roan, why?'

'At the time I thought it was necessary—fool that I was! But we'll get back to that. Megan, tell me first why you wanted to see me.'

'To talk about the accident.'

He backed away from her. 'Not again!'

'Yes.' She put her hand on his arm, and as always when the accident was mentioned, she felt it stiffen. 'I know what happened.'

His face was taut with strain. 'You've always known.'

'I've never known the truth. Roan. . . .' Her fingers stroked the bunched muscles and she wished that she could will him to relax. 'Why did you never tell me?'

'Let's change the subject.'

'Ann guessed. She told me you weren't to blame.'

'I was to blame,' he said harshly.

'No.' She tilted her head back to look at him. 'I know

about Larry. Also'—her voice was jerky—'about Tammy. I know they'd been drinking.'

She heard the hiss of breath. 'Ann told you that?'

'Larry did.'

'That's hard to believe. Why would he tell you?'

'I kind of forced it out of him.'

Roan smiled, briefly. 'I always said you were a determined woman!'

'Are you going to tell me about it?' she demanded.

'I don't know.' His eyes had left her and had gone to the vlei. His jaw was tight, his eyes aloof. A stranger might have thought he was watching the ducks, but Megan knew that he did not see them at all.

'Will you, Roan?'

And when he didn't answer, 'You've kept silent too long. You have to talk.'

He pushed a hand through his hair. 'Do you know how hard it is? Especially with you. You're Tammy's sister.'

I know, my darling. It's hard for me too.

'Perhaps that's why I'm the one who should hear it,' she said gently. 'You can't carry this with you all your life without talking about it.'

'It will always be there.' He looked distraught.

'I know, but you can't carry the burden alone. Share it with me, Roan.'

He was standing so close to her that she felt the shudder that ran through his body. Would he talk? He had brought her to the vlei to talk, though obviously not about the accident. She wondered what it was he had been going to say, but only fleetingly, for she knew that this moment would not come again. If Roan did not unburden himself now he might never do so.

'All right,' he said at last, and his voice was strained. 'Let's go and sit by those rocks there in the sun.'

They let their bodies curve with the shape of the

rocks. One of Roan's long legs was stretched out on the ground, the other was bent at the knee, and Megan could see the muscles beneath the tanned skin. As always she was aware of him physically; she wanted to touch him, to explore the shape of him. But this was a time for talking.

'It should never have happened,' he said after a while. As he began to talk, the story that unfolded was one that Megan already knew. There had been a party some distance away from Bronze Mountain. Tammy had gone there with Roan. There had been dancing, and Larry had cut in, asking Tammy to dance. They had spent the next hour together.

'My pride was dented a little, but that's about all,' Roan said. 'I'd had dinner with Tammy a few times, she was a lovely girl, but I'd already realised that she wasn't quite my type. She preferred Larry, and really they were more suited to each other.'

Roan had spent the time talking to others at the party. When he was ready to leave he went to tell Tammy. 'I thought she should go home with Larry if that was what she wanted.' He saw immediately that they had been drinking, and he decided that he would drive Tammy back to the resort himself. When Larry was ready to leave, one of the men would see to it that he did not drive himself.

Roan paused, and Megan felt herself tensing. This much of the story she knew. It was the rest that she needed to know.

'Brace yourself,' Roan said grimly.

Tammy had not wanted to leave the party. She had accused Roan of spoiling her fun, and Larry had been abusive.

'I insisted.' Roan was speaking so quietly now that Megan had to strain to hear his words above the breeze that ruffled the long grass and the water of the vlei. 'God in heaven, I should have let her stay!'

Roan had force-marched Tammy from the party Larry had said.

'I forced her to come with me. She didn't want to, but I took her by the arm and made her come. Can you understand, Megan?'—the face that turned to her was more tormented than she had ever seen it—'I thought that if Larry drove her back they might have an accident.'

'I do understand.'

'Tammy was furious,' Roan said after a long pause. 'I got her into the car and all the while she . . . she was shouting . . . she wanted to get back to the party, to Larry. I began to drive. She was pulling at my arm, trying to get me to turn back. We . . . we came to a bend, a sharp bend. . . .' He stopped.

'Go on,' Megan urged.

'I can't.'

'You must,' she insisted firmly, though the blood had frozen in her veins.

'Tammy was pulling at my arm. She managed to get to the steering wheel. I was stronger than she was, but . . . she kicked me. I was startled. In that moment she managed to pull the wheel the other way, and the car left the road.'

Silence fell as Roan stopped talking. A hand was over his eyes, as if he was trying to shut out the terrible picture that he had carried with him for the last months. Megan, shocked and trembling, had nothing to say.

And then, through her grief, Roan's despair got through to her. She had to help him. She put her hand on his arm. It was so rigid that it seemed as if the muscles might burst through the skin.

'It wasn't your fault,' she whispered softly.

He jerked around. 'My God, Megan, if I hadn't been so stubborn Tammy would be alive today!'

'You weren't stubborn. You were being responsible.'

'I insisted that she leave with me.'

'Only because you feared what would happen if she went home with a drunken man.'

'That's what I try to tell myself. It's what I've told myself since the day it happened. And all I can see is Tammy lying there. . . . And I know it didn't have to happen.'

Abruptly he got to his feet and strode to the edge of the water. He stood there, rigid in the way Megan had come to recognise. He stooped to pick up a stone, and hurled it across the water.

Then he came back to her. 'You know it all now.'

'Not quite all. Why wouldn't you drive with a passenger?'

Roan looked down at her a long moment—as if he was seeing through the skin and bones to her very soul, Megan thought. Then he squatted on the ground beside her.

'Guilt, I suppose.'

'You knew that you hadn't caused the accident. And you're an excellent driver. Even beneath that awful tarpaulin I knew that.'

'Guilt can be a terrible burden, Megan. For months I've tortured myself with the knowledge that Tammy would still be alive but for me.'

'And you punished yourself by not allowing yourself to drive with anyone else.'

'Something like that, I suppose.'

'Has talking helped, Roan? Will you be able to drive now?'

After a long moment he said, 'Yes.'

'That first day, you offered to drive me then. Why?'

He looked up at her. 'I wanted to get to know you. I wanted to talk to you.'

'And I didn't give you a chance. I've never forgiven myself for that.' She paused. 'And today?'

'I wanted to talk to you again. I brought you here to the vlei to talk. And now'—he looked towards the water—'I don't know if I can.'

'Try,' she prompted, trying to quell a sudden quivering inside her.

She saw him take a breath. He looked like a man who had made a decision. When he looked at her again his eyes were steady. 'I love you very much, Megan.'

Was it possible to feel quite so happy? 'I love you too,' she said softly.

'You told me so the other night and I threw it back at you.' He let out a groan. 'Fool that I was!'

'Why did you?'

'I'll tell you that too, but first I want to kiss you.'

He lowered himself on to the ground, close beside her, and drew her to him. He kissed her tenderly, yet hungrily, and she wished he would never stop.

When he paused to draw breath, she whispered against his mouth, 'It's like the first time, here at the vlei.'

'So much has happened since then. I've put you through hell, my darling Megan.'

'Because that's where you were yourself.'

'And you understood all along. Megan, my darling, I fell in love with you that first day, but I couldn't let myself love you.'

'Because of Tammy.'

'Yes.' She felt the breath that shuddered through him. 'At Shengala I wanted you so much, I've never desired a woman as I've desired you—but at the last moment I had to draw back.'

'And when I came to your cabin and told you I loved you?'

'The same thing. More than anything else I wanted to make love to you, but I had to send you away.'

'Still because of Tammy?'

'Not only Tammy. Megan darling, I've needed you so badly. And every time you were there for me. I was the one needing you all the time.'

Dimly she understood what he was trying to say. 'You couldn't accept that?'

'Somehow I couldn't. You were there for me every time, trying so hard to give me back my confidence. I needed you, but you never seemed to need me.'

'That's not true!' she protested.

'And then you got lost in the forest.'

'I needed you then.'

'That was the turning point,' Roan admitted.

'Did I have to get lost?' she asked incredulously. 'Was it necessary that I be in such desperate need?'

'No!' He cradled her to him, dropping kisses in a light path over her face before he went on talking. 'If that were the case I'd really be the worst kind of chauvinist. When Ann came to tell me you were missing I thought I'd go out of my mind! It wasn't hard to know why you'd run off. It took hours to find you in that dark forest. I had lots of time to think, and I realised what a fool I'd been.'

'Did you also realise that *I*'ve needed *you* all the time?' Megan asked softly. 'From the very beginning?'

'Have you? Have you really?'

'Do I have to prove it to you?' She smiled, reaching up shamelessly to draw his head down to hers again.

'I don't deserve this,' he said finally.

'You're rejecting me again?'

'I'll *never* reject you again.' He kissed her, hungrily and deeply. 'Will you marry me, Megan?'

Yes! Yes, yes, yes.

'What about Petra?' It was a question she had to ask before she could answer him, even though he had already told her that he had never made love to that girl and that she meant nothing to him.

He lifted his head, and his eyes were serious. 'Petra came to my cabin because I asked her to. I knew you were coming, and I didn't know what you wanted. I just knew that I couldn't handle your coming. I loved you so much, Megan, but I couldn't handle it, so I tried to scare you away.' He looked down at her. 'Can you forgive me?'

'If you make it worthwhile.'

He kissed her, thoroughly.

'That was almost worthwhile,' she grinned up at him.

'You're a witch, do you know that? A tantalising, adorable little witch. You haven't said if you'll marry me.'

'Yes, my darling Roan.'

His face was serious once more. 'Your parents—how will they feel?'

'Darling Mom and Dad, one day you'll love Roan as I do,' read the last mental letter that Megan would ever write from Bronze Mountain. 'There are things I have to tell you, other things that you will never know. But you'll love Roan. Once you've met him and know how happy he makes me, you'll love him too.'

Aloud she said, 'It won't be easy for them at first, but in time they'll understand.'

'You really think so?'

'I know it,' she said with sudden conviction.

'Will you marry me soon, Megan?'

'Yes!'

Roan nuzzled his chin against her hair. 'I've hurt you so much. I'm going to spend the rest of my life making it up to you.'

'Why not start now?' she suggested, and very satisfyingly, while the ducks swam on the vlei, Roan did just that.

BARBARA DELINSKY
Fingerprints

Carly Quinn is a
woman with a past.
Born Robyn Hart, she
was forced to don a new
identity when her intensive
investigation of an arson-ring
resulted in a photographer's death
and threats against her life.

Ryan Cornell's entrance into her life
was a gradual one. The handsome
lawyer's interest was piqued, and then
captivated, by the mysterious Carly—a
woman of soaring passions and a
secret past.

Take these
4 best-selling novels
FREE

Yes! Four sophisticated, contemporary love stories by four world-famous authors of romance FREE, as your introduction to the Harlequin Presents subscription plan. Thrill to **Anne Mather**'s passionate story BORN OUT OF LOVE, set in the Caribbean.... Travel to darkest Africa in **Violet Winspear**'s TIME OF THE TEMPTRESS....Let **Charlotte Lamb** take you to the fascinating world of London's Fleet Street in MAN'S WORLD....Discover beautiful Greece in **Sally Wentworth**'s moving romance SAY HELLO TO YESTERDAY.

Harlequin Presents...

The very finest in romance fiction

Join the millions of avid Harlequin readers all over the world who delight in the magic of a really exciting novel. EIGHT great NEW titles published EACH MONTH! Each month you will get to know exciting, interesting, true-to-life people .... You'll be swept to distant lands you've dreamed of visiting .... Intrigue, adventure, romance, and the destiny of many lives will thrill you through each Harlequin Presents novel.

Get all the latest books before they're sold out!
As a Harlequin subscriber you actually receive your personal copies of the latest Presents novels immediately after they come off the press, so you're sure of getting all 8 each month.

Cancel your subscription whenever you wish!
You don't have to buy any minimum number of books. Whenever you decide to stop your subscription just let us know and we'll cancel all further shipments.